MARJORIE DALEY

Fire Ground

For the firefighters in my life
Robert "Ninja Bob" Green, A/O, HFR
William "Bull" Daley, Captain, RVFD
Robert "Slim" Lambertsen, Chief, RVFD
Keith Lambertsen, Chief, RVFD
MSgt James Calvin, Assistant Fire Chief, USAF

Thanks for all the stories

Acknowledgement

So many people have helped with this book that I have lost count and possibly even forgotten names - I hope you know I appreciate your efforts! A special thank you to Robin Posey-Blue, Janet Perkins-Corbett, and especially Jennie Lawrence who gave me the courage to try.

Prologue

The fascination with fire had started when he had been young. He had been caught only one time while setting fire to his father's shed, and he had learned two things. The first was caution. He had been able to lie his way out then. The second was that fire had exciting consequences. At that young age, he had been unable to hear fire speak to him. It had just been pretty. As he grew older, he learned to listen to the words that fire spoke deep in his heart, asking to be freed. He had always been careful, starting fires safely, in barbeque grills or burn barrels. He tended them with care, listening, and learning. Fire wrapped its fingers of flame around his heart and seared him. The color, the smell, the dancing flames spoke to him in words only he understood.

For years, the controlled burns had been enough, but as he had biked down the dark and deserted road, he heard fire speak to him. He needed to see the color, the shape, and the smell of fire. He stopped his bike and fumbled in his pocket for the book of matches he always carried. Excitement flaring in his blood in an almost sexual craving, he pulled a match free and struck it.

The match flared briefly, the dainty light reflecting off his thin face. The tiny flame reflected itself in the dark hair that hung in a heavy lock over the man's forehead, making the red highlights dance. The smell of phosphorus stung his nostrils. He stared at the flame, transfixed. Flame shivered, almost died, and then grew back into life as he cupped one hand lovingly around it. It danced merrily in the slight breeze. He loved the very colors of the flame; blue, orange, red, and brilliant white. His breath caught; part of his brain filled with words of flame. He swayed with it. The Flame wanted to be bigger. It wanted to roar its defiance at a world that would control fire, not worship it. It bowed towards the bed of a hay-filled pick- up. Flame grew and became Fire. He could hear Fire talking to him.

A flick of his wrist and the match would land in the back of the pickup. The Flame would live. The Fire would live. He could be gone before anyone noticed. He knew the owner of the truck. Someone he had met long ago and struck up a cordial and mutual dislike. It would serve the owner right if he sacrificed the truck to his need for fire. He was very tired of setting fires in his grill. He needed something bigger. A place larger, more powerful, more majestic to reflect the power of Fire. He was no longer a boy to be discovered by nosy parents.

The match burned down to his fingers, and he dropped it with a curse and profound sorrow. Should he? Yes. Light another, the fire said. The truck would burn. The load of hay would blaze merrily. He did not like horses anyway. The second match flipped into the hay, guttered and went out. Flame cried in pain in his head, almost deafening him. With an exasperated sigh, he pulled two matches out of the book, stuck one behind the remaining matches so only the head stuck out. Then he lit the second and touched it to the first one. There was a hiss as the match caught. He laid it carefully down in a sheltered spot in the hay and climbed onto his bike to pedal away. As he hurried off, he heard the gentle whoosh of the matchbook and all the matches catching fire.

It would not do to be the first on the spot. They, the firefighters — the murderers of his beloved fire — they would be looking for the first person on the scene, the onlooker, the first 911 caller, to be the arsonist. He shivered at the thought of the word. "Arsonist." The power of fire was his to control and to terrify the people who angered him. He loved fire. It spoke to him in the bright red-orange language that only he understood. He would come back, do his job, no one would be the wiser, and he would still see the excitement and the drama that were his to control.

Chapter 1

At last, the fire engine was clean. The long sides gleamed in the station bay lights, the chrome on the pump panel shone as brightly as it had when it rolled off the assembly line two years ago. Even the tires were clean and blacked. The only thing not shiny were the hoses. No matter how clean the polyester weave was, hoses always managed to look dirty after their first few fires and being dragged through mud, soot, and across street tops.

Kenzie Stevenson fluffed her corkscrewed hair off her forehead, flicked out her rag, and sat down on the front of the engine where the bumper stuck out far enough to make a relatively comfortable seat. Her hair, the bane of her existence, was curly, and as a little girl, she had resembled Shirley Temple. She braided firmly down on duty days, but tendrils escaped and curled with great enthusiasm on the city's first, and so far, only, female firefighter.

"Tired?" Her best friend and station mate, John Barstow, sat down next to her. He leaned back with a sigh, and Kenzie looked at him fondly. Line firefighting was hard work.

"Been a long day. On days like this, I think of the big city stations that change shifts on the scene and almost never go back to the station. Then days like this don't seem so bad."

Kenzie reached down to polish an imaginary blemish on the already shiny winch on the front of the fire engine.

"Gas leaks in summer are sure a pain." JohnB, so called to differentiate him from Johnny on C shift, agreed and closed his eyes. Quiet companionship filled the warm summer night. That morning, a gas main had ruptured, and they had spent most of a sweltering morning in full turnouts making sure nothing went wrong while the gas company repaired the leak. It was standard protocol, but it was a sweaty experience.

This time, a Good Samaritan had purchased cold drinks for the entire shift, a relief after the lukewarm water stored in the engine for just such an occurrence. Kenzie's station had rolled off the gas leak straight into a kitchen fire and then to two medical assists. By now, it was well past bedtime, except the engine had to be ready for the next emergency.

Kenzie glanced around the engine bay to make sure everything was in order. Her dog, the one non-regulation item in the entire fire station, thumped his tail on the floor as she caught his eye. Flower was an accelerant detection dog, more commonly known as an arson dog. Like most professional dogs, he spent every minute of every day with his handler, including her duty days. He had a bed and a kennel in Kenzie's room and many willing hands to scratch his ears. It was, Kenzie figured, the doggy life of Riley and meant this fire station had a Labrador Retriever as a station mascot, instead of the traditional Dalmatian.

The radio speaker emitted a short series of clicks and then a deep burr. At the first click, Kenzie and JohnB had stopped, waiting silently. At the tone, keyed to their station, Flower hauled himself up with a groan and trotted to the door leading to Kenzie's room, waiting patiently. After seven years, he was well-versed in fire station protocol. The tone ended.

"Station One, dispatch. Toning out Engine One and Rescue One on a vehicle fire at 1946 East Pershing. Station one, vehicle fire at 1946 East Pershing. Time is 2106."

"It's showtime." JohnB hopped up and hauled Kenzie off the bumper. The other firefighters begin to converge on the bay, walking swiftly but not running. Too many accidents happened around fire stations and missing a fire because of a fall and broken leg on concrete was bad form. Kenzie headed to her room to put the waiting Flower into his kennel, then hurried back to suit up, the rumbling of the rescue truck's bay door adding wings to her feet.

The rescue crew responded first, taking control of the scene and letting the engine crew know what to expect. The rescue lieutenant could also call for other units if the emergency required more hands than were on the way. It took a little longer for the engine crew to get ready on the station end, but they stepped off the engine fully prepared to fight the fire, at which point the rescue crew suited up.

JohnB was almost ready; the apparatus operator/driver/engineer, Joey, right behind him, and the lieutenant was responding on the radio to dispatch. Kenzie kicked off her station shoes into her locker, just as the fifth engine crew, Kurt, slid up next to her.

"Bathroom," was all he said.

"Bummer." Kenzie could commiserate. She had been in the bathroom more than once when the tone went off. It was an uncomfortable experience.

The rescue truck pulled out to the street, paused for traffic, and then the siren began to scream as it turned east out of the station. Kenzie stepped into her fire boots with the bunker pants neatly folded down around the tops. She yanked up the pants and skinned into the braces. She pulled on her bunker coat and grabbed her helmet, hood, and gloves, and headed to the fire engine, beat by nanosecond by Kurt, the fastest dresser in the station. JohnB and Kurt, her jump seat crew, were already in their seats, carefully buckling their coats closed.

Firefighter movies aside, one never went anywhere without being properly suited up. There was no glory in being burned because you forgot to dress yourself properly. As the driver started the engine, they buckled their safety belts.

The engine rumbled out after the rescue truck within thirty seconds. Kenzie finished her suiting up by pulling a Nomex hood over her head, adjusting it carefully before pulling the facemask down around her neck, and buckling on her helmet. The faceplate on the helmet would stay up. With an air mask in place, the faceplate had almost no practical purpose—kept for the occasional eye protection and tradition, and it quickly got scratched.

It was a good indication, though, in a house of how hot a fire was. Melting faceplate was a disastrous sign. Last were heavy gloves. Kenzie smoothed them down, making sure they fit well. Then they had nothing to do but wait. As they approached the scene, the three craned their heads over the seat, brains kicking into emergency mode, sizing-up, a quick assessment that each firefighter did. The information they gathered would guide their actions, making their responses much quicker and safer.

"Second truck filled with hay fire we've had this month. Someone's got something against horses." JohnB observed.

The fire lit the sky in shades of red and orange with thick evil black smoke boiling over it and creeping along the ground before lifting into the night sky. The bed of the truck was burning fiercely, and Kenzie checked it off as probably lost. She leaned against the air pack, happy not to be squirming into it. On a vehicle fire, the jump seat crew rarely needed to wear their air packs since the smoke and heat were able to dissipate into the open air. Last in, first out, Kenzie slid out of the cab and pulled the booster line off the engine. It was small enough that one person could handle the stream.

"Charged." The driver (A/O) behind her yelled to let her know there was water in the hose. Kenzie pushed the nozzle opened, and water sprayed out. She aimed at the base of the fire in the bed of the truck and was immediately rewarded with white steam and gray smoke, signs of a fire going out. Within a minute, the fire was reduced to mostly smoke, the sign of incomplete combustion, and steaming stinking ruined hay. She cut off the flow and waited while the others pulled the load apart, spreading the hay bales on the ground. She opened the line again and gave them a complete soaking, just to make sure they were out.

From her vantage point, the fire had not destroyed as much of the truck as she had thought. The rear window had melted, but the fire had yet to spill into the interior. The bed was charred but not as bad as one would think. Fires burned upwards, and areas below the fire could be relatively untouched.

Hay was funny stuff. It could catch fire without warning and could reignite with great vigor. Given the green smell of the hay and the pickup's open bed, Kenzie doubted the fire was natural. Hay usually spontaneously combusted in a dusty, hot, enclosed building. The fire crew might get lucky and find evidence since the fire had been concentrated in the upper bales.

The lieutenant was questioning the owner when JohnB pointed out a partially burned matchbook with a match stuck sideways in it tumbled to the bottom of the truck bed. At that point, the fire became a crime. Proving a fire was incendiary was relatively easy. Proving the identity of the arsonist was the problem. Many arsons were crimes of convenience, and witnesses were few. They would call in the fire marshal, and Kenzie knew this was one fire she would not be investigating for her part-time job. On this fire, as a responding firefighter, there was too much conflict of interest for her to investigate this particular fire.

"Hey, Kenzie." A lanky man with dark hair walked over to Kenzie with all the assurance of the press within a restricted area.

"Hey, Gordo." Kenzie greeted an old acquaintance from college, now videographer for the local news station and freelance photographer.

"How's it going?"

"Busy. My fire senses say it's going to be a long night. Gas main leak, two fires, and a couple medicals, so far today."

"Fire senses? Anything like Spidey senses?" Gordo Ellis laughed.

"Except for the radioactive spider part."

"So, what caused the fire?" Gordo asked. Kenzie looked away to hide the rolling of her eyes. The press was a pain. Of course, they would ask the same question every time, and of course, she would reply with the same stock answer every time, friend or no friend.

"The fire is under investigation by the fire marshal. You'll have to ask at his office. Look, I've got to go clean up. See you later." Kenzie walked away, dragging the hose with her. Gordo danced a few steps to keep from being knocked over by the hose snaking past him.

On the periphery of the fire, she noticed a police officer she had not seen before leaning against his patrol car, watching her intently, arms crossed over a chest made even more substantial by his Kevlar vest. As their eyes met for a brief moment, he finger-combed dark hair back from his forehead, where it fell in messy waves. Kenzie snorted. Yet another man who was going to think she had to prove her worth. She was completely over proving herself to anyone.

JohnB waited by the booster line reel, rags in hand. He wrapped the rags around the hose, cleaned off a few feet. Kenzie pressed the rewind button on the reel and guided the hose onto the reel, sort of like loading thread on a bobbin. JohnB cleaned dirt, water, and gunk off the hose as it was loaded. Clean equipment lasted and did not fail at the worst possible opportunity. When she was finished, Kenzie climbed into the seat. JohnB and Kurt joined her.

"Man, I am one tired puppy dog." JohnB groaned as he sat back on the engine seat as much as possible, given that the air pack was housed as part of the seat and not very comfortable to lean against.

"I predict a house fire tonight. Two a.m." Kenzie said.

"Nah. A wreck or a heart attack. Saturday night, game on campus. Lots of drunks." Kurt stated.

"Game's over." John pointed out.

"Drinking isn't. Just getting started."

"Well, shee-it. It'll be all three." JohnB muttered.

"Don't be such a gloomy Gus. You're supposed to be the hotshot fire eater." Kenzie teased.

"Fires," JohnB stated, eyes closed, "don't barf all over you while you work."

"Good point." Kenzie grimaced.

"Man, am I hungry." Kurt, the station's bottomless pit and self-proclaimed refrigerator cleaner, commented with complete lack of appropriateness. JohnB rolled his eyes at Kenzie, who giggled. Only Kurt would think of food after discussing vomiting drunks.

Back at the station, the crew hung their bunker coats on designated spots on the cab. The driver had the primo spot, his bunker coat draped over the rear-view exterior mirror, and bunker pants directly in front of his open engine door. Helmets were set neatly on the shelf next to the station door, gloves crammed into the helmet. Kenzie climbed into the cab to make sure her air pack was ready to wiggle into and straightened out her harness to ensure it would be easy to put on. No need to waste time on the next call struggling to get into a twisted harness while the crew waited. Kenzie had had more than one nightmare along that line, especially during rookie school. Those were almost as fun as the naked-at-a-fire dreams.

Last of all, she carefully folded the bunker pants down over the boot tops and stepped into her station shoes. Everything was neat, clean and in its place. Kenzie could lay her hands on anything in the engine's storage compartments with her eyes closed. On the proverbial dark and stormy nights, or late-night calls before the adrenaline hit, she depended on the absolute neatness of the engine to quickly find what she needed.

Then the engine had to be cleaned and restocked, and the 1,000-gallon tank of water filled, making sure it was ready for the next run. At least the engine was still mostly clean. Otherwise, the firefighters would have to help Joey, the driver, wash and dry it. No firefighter worth the name wanted to be seen in a fire engine that was less than shiny.

"I hope Rescue didn't eat all the ice cream. I'm starving." Kurt rumbled and took himself off to the kitchen for a late-night snack. Kenzie went to her room to take care of her dog and collapse in a heap until the next call or morning, whichever came first.

One alcohol poisoned student later, Kenzie's shift was over. Sunday to sleep in, Monday to do cause-and-origin paperwork or maybe an investigation, and then on Tuesday, back to the station for another shift. She dragged herself out of the station and went home to work Flower and take a perfectly lovely afternoon nap. Life was good.

Chapter 2

The next duty day, a Tuesday, the engine crew was assigned to grocery shop for the shift. Breakfasts were eaten at home, dinners were leftovers, sandwiches, or brought by spouses. On an average shift, the main station meal was lunch, and one or two firefighters were detailed to shop and cook for the crew. Firefighters were usually exceptionally good cooks, and station meals were the cement that held a crew together. Kenzie had seen more than one crew fall apart when the crew lieutenant eliminated the lunch tradition. She had also seen a crew come together when a good cook was moved onto that crew.

Kenzie had decided before she applied for the fire service never to admit she loved to cook. Otherwise, she envisioned a fire career chained to the station stove, and she could imagine the jokes about the "little woman firefighter." The teasing, even without that label, had been annoying enough. She had even managed to ruin coffee on her first few shifts, and now she was relegated to clean up, which suited her just fine. The only firefighter she had ever cooked for was JohnB, and he had solemnly sworn to keep her secret.

Kenzie and JohnB went to the grocery store while the rest of the engine crew waited in the fire engine. Portable radios kept them in touch, so if an emergency occurred, they could respond and not be left behind as the engine pulled away. The two stood in front of the meat case, debating the merits of chicken versus pork chops for the station lunch.

Fellow shoppers glanced at the two, and their reactions were almost universal. At first, a small smile of appreciation for the fact that they were visible representatives of a valuable service. Then, the stock appreciative glance at JohnB. Then the eye slide to her, followed invariably by a double-take when people saw past her uniform and realized she was undeniably female. Even after ten years of service, her presence still came as a surprise to the townspeople.

Over the years, Kenzie had gone from resentment to amusement over the stares JohnB got wherever they went. He was tall, blonde, muscled, and Kenzie teased him about being Mr. July on firefighter calendars—the ones who posed in as little as possible casually draped across a shiny fire engine.

"Smoky mountain chicken. Bacon, cheese, chicken. What more could your stomach ask for?" Kenzie suggested.

"It's my arteries that I'm worried about. Smoky mountain chicken sounds like a heart attack special. How about pork chops smothered in onions?" JohnB replied. Kenzie made a face.

"Onions make you stink." Kenzie refused bluntly.

"Geez, Kenzie. Let's not be too direct." JohnB looked longingly at the pork chops. He was riding the rescue truck that night, which meant sleeping in the same suite as the rescue lieutenant instead of his private room where no one would complain. Perhaps a little courtesy was in order. "Okay, chicken." JohnB gave in with little graciousness.

"Good. I'll run an extra mile tomorrow, burn it out of my

arteries."

"Kenzie?" An older woman touched Kenzie's arm gently. Kenzie turned toward the speaker.

"Hey, Mrs. James." Kenzie's green eyes lit up as she smiled down at the older woman. "How are you?"

"I'm fine, dear. Paul and I were talking about you the other night. We haven't seen you in ages. You should come to dinner soon."

"I'd love to. I'm on duty tonight, but I can come another night."

"Tomorrow, about seven?"

"I'll be there. Can I bring anything?"

"No, dear. Just yourself." Mrs. James looked curiously at JohnB as she spoke. Kenzie mentally shook herself to remind her of better manners.

"JohnB, this is Mrs. James, this is John Barstow, my partner on the engine." As she made the introductions, the two shook hands.

"I've heard a lot about you, John." Mrs. James said. JohnB flashed her a brilliant grin that made the older woman's lips twitch in response.

"Nothing good, I expect," JohnB replied.

"Only in the beginning." Mrs. James patted his hand. Kenzie marveled at how everyone responded to her partner's easy charm. It occasionally made her life much easier, especially on rescues. Of course, beating off the fire groupies that followed him back to the station made her life harder. Nevertheless, it generally evened out in the end.

"Ouch." JohnB's smile grew rueful. Kenzie grinned at her friend.

"Your reputation precedes you, Stinky."

"Kenzie dear, I have to hurry home. John, it was nice to meet you." She turned to the younger woman. "Tomorrow at seven?"

"I'll be there." The two watched as she turned the corner down the frozen food aisle and then gathered the rest of their groceries. They had made it through an entire shopping expedition without being toned out on a fire or rescue. Many times, they had had to leave groceries in the cart and rush out. Lunch then usually became frozen pizza, warmed between calls, or eaten cold. Kenzie and JohnB went through the checkout and joined the rest of the crew waiting in the fire engine.

The next evening, Kenzie wrapped up her part-time job as an origin-and-cause investigator and hurried home to shower off the day's grime and sweat. She chose jeans and a t-shirt, knowing neither James would expect formality, not to mention that her wardrobe did not run to many girly clothes. The long, hot summer day would fade into a cool evening, so it was nice enough to walk the short distance to the James' house. With any luck, she would be walking off some of Mrs. James' famous ooey-gooey desserts on the way home.

Kenzie grabbed a sweatshirt and called her dog to her side. He responded immediately; his manners as always impeccable. His manners were no accident, but the result of hundreds of hours of training. Kenzie rarely left the dog behind, and the constant companionship built their relationship into something more than a dog and owner. She considered him as much a partner as JohnB. Because her life would never depend on Flower, unlike a K-9 and handler relationship, Kenzie would always be the alpha leader, the head bitch, as JohnB called her, and Flower the loyal subordinate.

The walk was a little over a mile, and both thoroughly enjoyed the activity. Dog and woman went down a tree-lined street and ducked down an alley as a shortcut. Kenzie had made this walk a thousand times throughout her graduate degree and only once, on her first visit, had she used the front door.

Once she was in the James' back yard, she raised her eyebrows over a well-used mountain bike leaning against the house. She sincerely doubted either James had taken up biking, especially not the type of biking requiring heavy-duty shock absorbers and seriously treaded tires. Flower sat down in front of the bike in arson dog alert posture. Whoever rode the bike must have run over a dribble of gas.

"Good dog, Flower." She handed him a treat and went up the steps to the door. "Hi, Mrs. James. Hey, Doc." Kenzie banged on the back door, opened it, and leaned in.

"Come in, Kenzie." Doc James called out. Kenzie stepped into the bright kitchen and paused at the sight of a stranger sitting at the kitchen table. Just like in a child's game of matching, Kenzie could figure out what went with what, and the mountain bike was definitely this stranger's. Looks-wise, he was most definitely a James. Kenzie pulled her eyes away from him with no little effort and greeted her hosts. Mrs. James stood near the stove, stirring something that smelled divine. Doc James smiled at Kenzie from the kitchen table.

"Hi, Doc. Mrs. James." Kenzie greeted them. Her eyes drifted back to the unknown James, and she felt time stretch subjectively. Tall like his father with a slim build and dark hair. Lean face with dark brown eyes that had a hint of laughter underneath the reserve. There the similarity ended. While the elder James' and Kenzie were dressed casually, he was dressed in chinos and a collarless shirt, pressed, unless she missed her guess and quite possibly starched.

Kenzie only ironed when collars rolled, and shirts gaped because the placket wrinkled into a thin strip. Hair so dark brown as to be almost black, unlike both James's who had been grey as long as she had known them. His hair was cut short on the sides and then spiked on top. He looked altogether like one of the models from a hair salon magazine. He was remarkably good looking; something Kenzie normally avoided in a man. Personality was greatly preferred over looks any day, in her books.

The door slammed shut on her foot. Apparently, time had not stretched too far, she thought with a grimace. Doc was just rising to his feet. The stranger's lips twitched, and the humor hiding in his eyes lit them up as she extracted her foot and held the door open for Flower.

"Come on in, Kenzie, dear." Mrs. James said with a smile.

"No need to let in the flies, Kenzie." Doc held out his arms for their customary hug. Kenzie complied. Stepping back, Doc grinned at her. Somehow, she doubted either older James had missed that little episode in the door when heavenly music played in her ears. She probably still looked stunned.

"I brought Flower. Is he ok in the house?" She asked a stock question, and Doc James gave his stock nod. Flower looked up at her and at her nod; he gave his customary tail wag to the people he had met before and then gazed solemnly at the James' son. Then, unexpectedly, he went to him, tail wagging, and offered his paw. The man took it with a smile.

"I'd say you've made a friend. I've never seen him do that before." Kenzie said and snapped her fingers, pointing to an out of the way spot on the kitchen floor. Flower went to lie down in a corner, eyes on his person. Flower took himself and his job very seriously. In Flower's opinion, arson dogs had no time for typical doggy enthusiasm.

"Kenzie, this is our son, Lee. Lee, this is Kenzie Stevenson, and you've already met Flower." Doc introduced Kenzie to the stranger, pride evident in his voice. Lee stood up with a gracefulness that made Kenzie feel awkward. His hand was large and strong and warm without being clammy. Kenzie smiled inanely at him.

"Lee transferred to the police department down here about two months ago. Haven't been able to get him to move out." Doc grumbled good-naturedly, but Kenzie was quite sure Doc and Mrs. James were not unhappy to have their only child home.

"It's just Mom's cooking. I'm tired of Top Ramen and pizza." Lee's voice was deep and just as attractive as the rest of the package.

"Oh, you. I'll put that on the menu if you promise to move out so I can have my craft room back." Mrs. James gave her son a quick one-armed hug, the other hand holding a basket of home-cooked dinner rolls. "If you'll carry everything to the dining room table, we can eat."

Mrs. James handed Lee the basket and then quickly organized a procession of food until pork chops and onions, broccoli covered with cheese, rolls, and iced tea graced the table. Kenzie wondered just how much of her conversation with JohnB that Mrs. James had overheard as this was the exact meal they had discussed in the grocery store.

Doc must have arteries made of stone by now since down-home cooking was what Mrs. James served at every meal Kenzie had ever eaten at the James' house. Kenzie found herself seated across the table from Lee. She frowned slightly, a whisper of memory tickling her brain.

"I know you. You were at the truck fire on Pershing Road. But your hair was different." Kenzie finally put all the pieces together. He had been the one staring at her. Lee reddened and ran his hand over his hair.

"A little ...er ... mishap with hair gel and badly needed haircut." At his words, Doc snorted. "Sorry about staring. I figured you must be Kenzie." He smiled at her, and Kenzie managed not to spill, or drool, or any of the other one hundred most embarrassing things to do in front of a cute guy.

"How's business?" Doc asked. Kenzie made a face.

"Going too well. We got back from our annual training session in Florida this year, and we've had five out of town fires since. Flower and I haven't been home three days in a row since April." Kenzie looked down at her plate and sighed. "Flower's starting to slow down, and the work is getting to him. They are supposed to slow down our schedule since the ATF is just finishing a new arson dog school."

"What's the job expectancy for an arson dog?" Lee asked.

"About eight years. He's seven now. I'll retire him in a year or two. But I've been trying not to think about that day."

"You going to get another dog?"

"I don't know. I'll have to find another house if I get one. Two Labs in a townhouse are a little much." Kenzie glanced over to where Flower lay on the floor, now collapsed to his side, legs extended. He could take up more space than any dog she had ever met. Two of them would pretty much turn her townhouse into a kennel. "This is great, Mrs. James." She looked appreciatively at her plate. Home cooking and she did not have to do a thing, except the dishes. "I think we have an arsonist on our hands. There've been about two fires of suspicious origins in trucks filled with hay over the last month.

Seems to be random, so far, so I figure we've got a firebug."

"We got briefed the other day by your fire marshal. Probably some kid." Lee offered.

"Maybe. Kids usually don't set cars on fire unless they steal them first. Walk-by arsons are more adult, a revenge sort of deal. On the first fire, we found two burned matches as the incendiary device. Kids usually light and run. This arson run smells of an adult with an ax to grind."

"Kids are getting pretty sophisticated these days, what with the internet and cop shows six times a night on TV." Lee pointed out. Kenzie shrugged.

"Maybe the ATF needs to update their profiles, but until then, this is an adult. Unfortunately, unless we're lucky and Joe Public spots him, this kind of arson is pretty impossible to stop. I guess that's job security. Oh, man, Mrs. James." Kenzie's voice went soft as the older woman set down a plate of gooey chocolate and cream-filled dessert. The others laughed at her expression.

"I don't know how you stay so thin, Kenzie, the way you love chocolate." Mrs. James said with a smile.

"Didn't you ever watch Emergency? Firefighters don't have time to eat. Plus, this is the only place I ever get desserts like this."

"See why I don't want to move out?" Lee exchanged grins with Kenzie, one of complete accord with the importance that chocolate holds in any meal.

After the meal, Kenzie helped to wash the dishes and clean up with Lee's cheerful assistance. Mrs. James left them strictly alone in the kitchen, a fact that both embarrassed and tickled Kenzie. What Lee thought of it, she had no clue, but he rose to the occasion with a grin. She enjoyed Lee's quiet, often ironic, sense of humor. He was funny and had a wealth of stories to share and interested in her without dominating the conversation. Kenzie found him a breath of fresh air.

In her experience, most guys were either intimidated by her profession or determined to undermine her status with belittling remarks. They wanted to prove that they, too, were brave enough to run into a burning building – even the ones who Kenzie was sure could not deal with a wasp in the house. She was leery of dating other firefighters or even law enforcement personnel. Too much possibility for conflict, and too often, law enforcement and fire service were obsessed with their jobs. While Kenzie could hold her own with the most obsessed, she enjoyed more than just that narrow subject. This one, this one might just be worth taking a chance on. When the chores were done, they joined the older James's in the living room and talked for a little longer before Kenzie's long day began to catch up with her. The three escorted her to the back door.

"Kenzie dear, I made this especially for you." Mrs. James held out a gel candle in a bowl. Kenzie managed not to groan, although it was a near thing. Gel candles were an obsession with Mrs. James, and Kenzie had at least a dozen at home. Lee's childhood bedroom was now Mrs. James' craft room, presently turned back to his room, and Kenzie was surprised he could find a spot big enough to lie down. The last time she had been in the room, candle making equipment had covered every horizontal surface, and the closet had burgeoned with still more stuff. Kenzie held up the bowl to the light. Inside was a tiny fire department, complete with a black Lab sitting outside.

"Thank you so much. I'll never be able to burn this one."

"I can always make another one, dear. Just keep the fig-urines." Mrs. James said, placing one arm around Kenzie for a squeeze. Behind his mother, Lee rolled his eyes at Kenzie. She bit the inside of her lip to keep from laughing.

"Thank you for dinner, Mrs. James, Doc. Lee, it was good to meet you at last. I expect I'll be seeing you on scene." Kenzie nodded to Lee. Mrs. James glanced from Kenzie to Lee. Kenzie called Flower to her side.

"Lee, walk Kenzie home, would you?" Kenzie shot Mrs. James a vaguely suspicious look, which the older woman missed as she was bending over, very innocently petting Flower good-bye. Kenzie was not sure she wanted a matchmaker. Some things were better off handled independently.

"It's over a mile. Two miles round trip." Now that was a stupid statement. Kenzie kicked herself. Lee could surely do simple math.

"It would be my pleasure, Mom." Lee's voice was deadpan. "In two miles, I can walk off some of this dessert." With the barest glimmer of a wink at Kenzie, Lee reached past her and pushed open the screen door.

"Let's go, Flower. Good night. Thank you. I had a wonderful time." Kenzie called as the older couple waved good-bye. The door shut, leaving only a narrow strip of light on the grass. Kenzie had the sneaking suspicion that she would see the curtains twitching if she turned around.

"You don't have to walk me home. I don't mind the walk, and Flower is a great deterrent for most criminal minds."

"I can see that." Lee's voice rippled with laughter as they looked at the dog that had abandoned dignity for a good roll in the grass. The dog looked up at them from upside down, tongue hanging out of his mouth and legs akimbo.

"He'll lick the bad guys to death. Geez, Flower. Get up." She patted the dog to let him know she still loved him even when he was ridiculous. "Your bike?" She gestured towards it.

"Sure is. I'm discovering most of the trails I rode on as a kid are now through someone's McMansion."

"There are some good ones up in the mountains, and the green belt is great for a Sunday ride." Kenzie offered. Lee took the candle from her and carried it carefully.

"Haven't had time to go up to the mountains yet. Hopefully, before summer is over." Lee answered. They walked across the dark yard and down the alley in comfortable silence.

"How did your dog get such a ...." Lee's voice trailed off.

"Sissy name? My niece. His name is Berkshire Farms' Midnight Sun, but when I explained his job was to be a good smeller, she thought I meant he would smell good, like Flower the Skunk in Bambi. She was only four." Kenzie shrugged. "It was as good a nickname as any." She shoved her hands in her sweatshirt pockets, and they walked in silence for a few driveways. "You like being home?"

"Yeah. I am planning on moving out." Lee's voice held a tinge of embarrassment. "The police department is chronically understaffed, and I haven't had time to look for anything."

"I don't think your folks mind. Except for maybe your mom not having her craft room."

"Geez, I expect to wake up encased in gel." He snickered, and Kenzie joined in. "You know, they're getting old." His voice was soft. Kenzie thought of her own parents, five hours away in a different state.

"Shock, isn't it? I went home a few months ago, and my dad's completely grey." Kenzie sighed. Lee nodded. They turned down her street.

"I thought you'd be on a first-name basis with my folks."

"They've been Doc and Missus ever since my undergrad days, and I'd feel strange calling them anything else." Kenzie gestured towards the end townhouse. "This is my place. Thanks for walking us home. You going to be ok on the way home? I could walk you back."

"And then what? We walk each other home until we drop of exhaustion?" He crinkled the corners of his eyes, and Kenzie felt her stomach spiral away from her. What did it matter if he dressed more nicely than she did and actually styled his hair? Lee handed back the candle and stood smiling down at her. The silence stretched into uncomfortableness.

"The townhouse four doors down is for rent." Kenzie blurted.

"Is it now?" Lee replied with a thread of laughter in his voice. Kenzie wished she could kick herself for being so obvious. They stood for a few more endless seconds. Kenzie wondered what to say. Everything she could think of sounded stupid. Finally, Lee broke the silence.

"See you on the streets." She watched his tall form walk away down the darkened street. Kenzie leaned on the bumper of her truck, watching him go. Amazing to have been Doc's student for four years and a friend for five more without ever having met Lee. For years, he had been stationed in the north of the state, working the big city. She had been at home in another state on the rare occasions that he visited his parents. Nice guy. His lean form disappeared around the corner. He had not looked back.

Kenzie grimaced and balanced the candle where the street-light shone through it. It looked like the fire station was on fire. She shivered unaccountably and unlocked her door, Flower beside her. The house was quiet after the evening's gaiety.

Chapter 3

The next morning, Kenzie rolled out of bed, staggered into sweats and running shoes, and went for an early morning run. She would never be as strong as her brother firefighters, and to make up for that, she trained ruthlessly—walking, running, lifting weights, and biking. She had gone through hell to become a firefighter, and she hated it when people thought she had been hired to meet a quota instead of being capable. Her hire might have started as a quota, but she had earned the right to be a firefighter the hard way, one fire, one rescue, one day at a time.

Running was not her favorite activity, but her goal was to always score in the at least lower levels of the men's required physical activity times. That way, she did not look quite so like a pampered minority. When she and Flower returned home, she showered up and went to her upstairs office. It was paperwork day today, a chance to catch up on her reports.

Like most firefighters, Kenzie held down a second job on her off days. In her case, she had trained as an origin-and-cause investigator, formally called an arson investigator. Since fires were caused by more than arsonists, origin-and-cause was more exact.

Flower was her partner in this profession. Years of training and money had gone into Flower to turn him into a walking nose. He could identify dozens of different materials, like gasoline, that were commonly used to start fires and was constantly training to detect more.

His abilities made her life much easier, quickly, and efficiently locating a fire's origin, especially when someone had used something to make the fire burn more quickly and spread with a vengeance. Because fire burned up, not down, there were many times pools of liquid underneath the melted debris left by a fire, and that puddle left a distinct odor to a trained and sensitive nose.

An insurance company owned Flower and used the team to investigate claims. They also sold his and Kenzie's services to municipalities that could not afford a permanent accelerant detection dog. On any fire scene contracted by the insurance company, her job was to determine what had caused the fire.

If it was arson, law enforcement would be brought in. If it was accidental, she would document it for insurance purposes. Insurance payments depended on her reports. In the case of fires caused by appliances or other equipment, the data would be fed into a national database. If a specific source caused enough fires, for instance, a particular dryer make and model, that model would be recalled. It was hard work with lots of head-scratching and report writing. Kenzie loved it. There was nothing quite like solving puzzles.

She pulled the file on the latest fire out of her filing cabinet and opened it. Reams of computer-generated notes and scribbled handwritten ones filled the folder. This one was going to be a doozy, although Flower's special skills had not been needed. There were too many hydrocarbons on a vehicle fire, like gasoline and oil, and too many parts like seats made of petroleum by-products, for him to pick out any one source.

Kenzie spread out her notes. The son had parked his father's brand-new pickup truck in an angled space next to the family garage. He had, he said, left it in gear and turned off the engine. A short time later, it had somehow and mysteriously caught fire and, as the dashboard burned, had shorted out the electrical system. The engine had started, and the truck rolled off the pad, through a wood fence, across the backyard, ricocheted off the tree, and through the fence and down a slight hill to the neighbor's house. At that point, it had buried itself in the neighbor's back porch.

Fire had followed the vehicle, making the path extremely clear. The neighbor, thinking someone was trying to break in, had run out of the house with a shotgun, only to find his much-hated neighbor's car burning on his porch. Things had gone from bad to worse at that point. It was just fortunate that this had not turned into a murder investigation as well. Station five had had to wait for law enforcement to disarm the enraged neighbor before they could respond to the fire. Kenzie wondered if Lee had been on that call.

Kenzie shook her head to clear it of visions of Lee. She had seen him once, well twice, for heaven's sake. Focus. Car fire.

To complicate matters, Son had taken the truck without Father's permission, and the two were barely on speaking terms. Kenzie suspected the discord just might have predated the fire. So, her job was to determine if Son had set the car on fire, hoping to annoy Father, if Father had set the car on fire for insurance purposes, or if this was all just an interesting series of coincidences. She doubted the fire had been aimed at the neighbor. The entire chain of events was just too random.

The truck's worst damage had been in the passenger compartment, and Kenzie could trace where the fire had burned into the dashboard and the electrical system. These types of fires burned so quickly that the plastic from the dashboard melted, ran down to the floorboards, and covered the evidence without destroying it. She had found half-burned cigarettes in the ashtray under the melted dashboard. The front seat showed the worst damage, an ash ringed badly burned hole deep into the seat cushion.

Automobile cushions were made of petroleum byproducts and once ignited, would burn fiercely. The damage could sometimes appear to be caused by a liquid petroleum-based accelerant, such as gasoline, when the cause was simply a lit match or dropped cigarette on a seat cushion.

The interviews had been a bust. The son had admitted to having cigarettes in the car but had sworn he had not put a lit cigarette or match on the seat. The father had snarled that he wasn't at fault because he had not driven the truck in the two days previous to the fire. There was no evidence of an accelerant in the cab. Kenzie had not found any indication that the family was in arrears on the truck payments.

Reluctantly, she decided on a preliminary verdict of fire of unknown origin. Short of resorting to lead-lined hoses, she could not get the son to admit to passive-aggressive behavior of any sort. The insurance company would have kittens about the settlement. Not her problem, Kenzie reminded herself. Her job was to uncover the facts. What happened next was up to the adjustors and lawyers.

Kenzie picked and chose her words very carefully. She was too much a veteran of what hair-splitting the lawyers could and would do to win a case. She recalled a case where the lawyer, an idiot in Kenzie's considered opinion, had suggested Flower's abilities were witchcraft. After Flower had demonstrated his talents to an enthusiastic and admiring jury, the case had been dropped, and the homeowner was later charged with insurance fraud.

In a few days, the lab report that tested for accelerants would be returned, providing more concrete evidence one way or the other, and Kenzie could wrap up the report. She stretched and filed everything away. Too bad she could not keep the neighbor's interview. It was a masterpiece of invective. She reread it, chuckling, and then put it away with the rest. Time to go work out Flower's nose.

He had the technique down now, a dozen fires later. Light, throw, and bike away. No one was the wiser. He had found a pair of thin leather gloves to keep from spreading fingerprints all over the crime scene. Crime scene. Not crime scene. The scene of power.

It was even easy to toss a box of matches under a leaking engine, and that was an exciting fire. Flame crept up to the engine, and then whoosh, fire everywhere. Black smoke rose like a beckoning finger. Fire is here. Fire lives.

At home, he experimented with new and better ways to start fires. Incendiary devices, the internet called them. Ways to create a hotter fire that would catch more rapidly and burn more fiercely. In the past, the fires he set in his bar-be-que had been easily explained away—he was simply burning personal papers with a clumsy incendiary device of lighter fluid. This new fire-setting was far more exciting and fulfilling. He was learning to control the very thing that controlled him, the need to burn. The fires and the response- the fire engines, the furor, especially the press coverage- made him feel powerful. He always came back to the scene, but no one would ever guess it was him.

At first random, his fires became the vessel of revenge to everyone he felt had slighted him. He took care to set the fires randomly. One day, the east side of town and the nasty old lady librarian who had shushed him in the library in front of his 3rd grade crush. Another, on the west side, a car whose paint color he disliked. It was so random that he was unpredictable. He was the god of fire.

Kenzie stretched out in the recliner in the station day room, trying to keep her eyes open after a Sunday firehouse meal of epic proportions. Good things they did not eat like that every day or they'd all waddle to fires. Flower lay beside her chair on his comfy bed, dreaming of chasing something particularly appealing.

Equally somnolent firefighters snored in their rooms or watched TV. She could hear the dulcet tones of NASCAR from the next room and was very glad that whoever designed the fire station took into account that while firefighters may all live together, they did not always like the same entertainment.

The speakers located in every room clicked on, and what activity there was came to a halt, someone muting the TV. The sound of an open mike was followed by the two-tone series of notes. Kenzie groaned. It would be nice for the call to be a medical. That way, the medics could haul their full stomachs to the emergency while the engine crew stayed put and happily digested.

"Station One, dispatch, toning out on kitchen fire at 2734 Oak Street. Kitchen fire at 2734 Oak Street. Time out 1335." With groans, all the firefighters pulled themselves up and walked quickly into the bay. No one ran since running led to injuries. Fire poles had gone the same way; too many firefighters sliding down had broken ankles and legs. At a quiet order, Flower went to his kennel, and Kenzie pushed the door shut before following her brother firefighters into the engine bay.

"Dispatch, Station One. We are responding to a kitchen fire at 2734 Oak Street. Time is 1336." The big bay doors rattled open as the first driver out the station door pressed the bay door opener. The rescue truck siren began to scream as they reached the main road. Kenzie pulled on her bunker pants and coat, grabbed her gloves, helmet, and mask, and headed for the engine. She settled in beside Kurt, and then JohnB swung into the cab with a big grin. JohnB lived for fires.

As one, the three firefighters squirmed into air packs in harnesses that were integral to the seats. They had not needed them on a car fire because, odd weather conditions notwith-standing, the smoke drifted away, but in a house, the smoke had nowhere to go, hence the air and face mask. Kenzie ran her hands under each strap, setting them comfortably, then buckled the hip belt with a groan.

Fingers automatically sought out one of her most important pieces of equipment, her PSD or personal safety device, which sensed motion. Once it was turned on, a thirty-second seces-sion of motion or being held horizontal would trigger the alarm. The alarm sounded a steady beeping guaranteed to drive the wearer insane if it wasn't an emergency, and possibly the only way station mates could find a downed firefighter in a smoky, dark building. Kenzie flipped hers on.

Kenzie pulled her Nomex hood on, settling it to frame her face and carefully tucking her curls under the edges, where they wouldn't interfere with the seal on her mask. The mask she left dangling around her neck. She turned around almost as one with her jump seat crew so she could see what was coming. The rescue crew reported smoke but no visible flames in a cleared building. Kenzie breathed a sigh of relief.

Searching a smoky, burning house for victims was a vital part of the job but was never a good thing to have to do. They were supposed to be getting special infra-red goggles to help them find downed bodies from the outside, thereby eliminating crawling and feeling with outstretched hands. Still, so far, neither the city council nor the county commissioners had approved the purchases.

Smoke billowed out of the house in an oddly calm way, wafting in the air currents. The smoke would boil out in a fully involved fire, rising to form sometimes fantastic shapes. One could read the devil or dragons into the clouds. Deep down within their secret and superstitious hearts, firefighters believed the fire was a living beast, and there was nothing it liked more than to destroy.

As the engine rounded the corner, they could see a distraught young man was seen jump up and down and gesticulate wildly to the lieutenant. The engine stopped at the fire hydrant down the street from the house. JohnB climbed out of the seat and pulled a five-inch supply hose from the back of the engine. He wrapped it once around the hydrant and dropped to his knees to begin connecting the hose to a hydrant, using tools stored in a bag fastened to the hose. Kenzie could see JohnB unscrewing the hydrant cover with a two-handed motion that wasted no effort. He was the fastest hydrant man in the state, a fact proven at timed trials during firefighter challenges.

The driver pulled slowly down the street, laying hose behind the engine. They came to a stop at the house. The engine lieutenant swung down out of the seat while the remaining jump crew leaped out with well-trained precision and went to get equipment. The driver climbed out and put a hose clamp on the hose. This clamp would stop the water from blasting through the entire half-mile of hose stored in the engine's hose bed.

The resulting explosion of hose from the hose bed would be a spectacular display of carelessness. It would, of course, be the one mishap captured for perpetuity in the national firefighter magazines. The driver then went to work, disconnecting the supply hose from the remaining line in the hose bed and attaching it to the pump pane. He then adjusted the valves on the pump panel.

The levels and gauges would regulate the supply of water so that the firefighters on the other end wouldn't find themselves on a crazed, over-charged hose or dripping water from a pressureless line. He finished pressure calculations using his hand as a calculator, each joint and knuckle a different value. By working the different pressures and water demands on his hand, he could accurately and rapidly set the valves. No need for a calculator if a well-trained apparatus operator was on shift.

"Charging," JohnB yelled as he opened the hydrant, turning the 5-sided bolt on top with a 2-foot wrench, and the flat hose suddenly filled with water and became rock hard up to the hose clamp. JohnB moved down the line to the hose clamp and carefully released it by stomping on one side. The clamp fell safely open with a clang. A hose clamp coming off a charged hose could break bones.

As the hose was being laid and charging, Kenzie pulled on her mask, put one hand over the mask's out valve, and inhaled. The mask sucked tight to her face. The seals were good. She pulled her helmet back on and buckled it. Then Kenzie and Kurt pulled an attack line from the engine's bed and headed into the house. At the door, they dropped to their knees and advanced through the thick smoke. Kenzie cursed poor housekeeping as she rammed her knee into a book in the middle of the floor. She winged it out of the way and kept crawling.

Once in the kitchen, the source of the smoke became relatively easy to pinpoint. The oven was billowing smoke out the partially opened door. Flames licked at the cabinets and had already caught papers on the countertop on fire. Kenzie opened the hose's fog nozzle, and the smoke died away as the source of the fire was soaked, then sprayed the countertop and cabinets. They tried very hard not to cause more water damage than was necessary, but as the charred papers flew up and were plastered to the wall by water, Kenzie figured the owner would have a heck of a time getting all the soot off.

The two firefighters exchanged glances with each other, and Kenzie reached into the oven and pulled out what had been a pair of sneakers. All the plastic was melted onto the bottom of the oven. Kurt sprayed once more to make sure the plastic was out. It was new oven time for someone, maybe even a new kitchen. Cooking off all that plastic could be highly carcinogenic. It was new shoe time as well. The shoe leather was charred. Trickles of smoke floated in gentle spirals from the linings. Kenzie was glad to have her mask on. Nothing stank quite like cooked sneakers, except possibly microwaved sneakers.

Kenzie pursed her lips as she surveyed the shoes, and then the two walked back out of the house, carrying the mistreated shoes with them. A trail of water leaking from the hose marked their passage. Once out of the house, they found an audience of neighbors. Kenzie dropped the shoes on the pavement, and the two pulled down their masks.

"I'd say these are well done." Kurt grinned. Kenzie snickered at his expression. It had probably taken Kurt the whole walk back through the house to come up with that one. Brains were not his strong suit. The owner of the shoes did not smile back.

"JohnB, Kurt. Go ventilate the house. Kenzie, take a look around and make sure everything is ok." The lieutenant ordered, and the three dispersed. JohnB and Kurt would carry huge fans to place in the doorway to push air into the house, making the house's air pressure greater than the air pressure outside. Smoke would then be pushed out of the house as the air within the house tried to come to equilibrium. The technique was known as positive pressure ventilation or PPV and worked a lot more effectively than the old fans of yesteryear that tried to suck smoke out.

Kenzie went around to open a door on the other side of the house to let out the smoke. It was far more fun to break windows, but insurance companies frowned on excessive and unnecessary damages. Positive pressure ventilation would clear out the smoke quickly and make the house relatively livable again. Kenzie checked the kitchen to ensure the fire had not spread within the cabinets or walls and then went out to help put the hoses away.

"I feel really stupid." The man was saying to the lieutenant.

"It's not the first pair of broiled shoes we've seen, and it won't be the last. All in a day's work." The lieutenant replied. Plus, Kenzie thought to herself, it makes for great stories.

"Hey, you're a girl." A teenage girl stepped off the sidewalk and walked to Kenzie, who nodded with a smile. There were stars and a serious case of fire engine envy in the girl's eyes. "How'd you get to be a firefighter?"

"Finish school, stay in shape, and apply. Then have lots of

persistence. It's a great job." She glanced around at the activity on the fire ground. She'd have a few minutes for a small bit of public relations. "Come on. I'll show you around." Kurt and JohnB were cleaning off the hoses and laying them on the hose bed. Joey gave the girl a quick tour of the pump panel and then a peek through the compartments, all organized with military efficiency. As they drove off, the girl waved.

"Another recruit?" JohnB yelled over the engine.

"Maybe. She seemed more interested in the engine than in you. For once." Kenzie grinned at JohnB.

"Oh, my broken heart. Jailbait is not my love interest. Hey, good thing we already ate. The smell was enough to gag even the Bottomless Pit there." JohnB nodded at Kurt.

"Not me. There are leftovers in the fridge. I'm starved." Kurt returned without a flicker of a smile.

JohnB and Kenzie exchanged looks, and she smothered a giggle. Kurt was the best straight man in the world. He never took offense at any practical joke and never entirely caught on until it was too late.

Back at the fire station, while the driver washed the engine, the engine crew pulled the used hoses off the truck, drained them, and hung them on the hose dryer, a long arm raised to the top of the bay let the hoses dry. That way, they would not mildew, or rot and the crew could check them for damage.

Kurt and JohnB replaced the hoses with stored hoses, joking as they connected the hoses to the engine. They were in the process of changing over to rubber jacketed hoses since there was no need to hang and dry them, a chore that inspired firefighters to learn to put out as many fires as possible with a booster line. But yet again, the city had yet to fork over the funds. Fires were hard on equipment, and maintaining it was expensive enough without moving to the newest designs.

The white police car in front of the fourth townhouse down from hers was a new addition to the neighborhood. Kenzie noticed it several days later as she came home from a long day. Lee? Her interest brightened for a moment, and then the last twenty-four hours caught up with her. It had been a busy night of accidents and people with week old symptoms looking for free medical treatment.

She had spent the day investigating a shed fire, an insurance claim of nightmare proportions because of, according to the owner, a priceless and irreplaceable collection of tools stored within. She wearily slogged to her door, up the stairs to her bedroom, and collapsed on her bed. Flower could take care of himself for a few minutes. She had showered at least three times in the last twenty-four hours, and another shower could wait a little longer as well.

Kenzie woke with a start. Not another blasted med call. She sat up in confusion. What was it? The dog. Flower had barked. And something else. The doorbell. At that thought, the bell rang again. She staggered down the stairs and to the door. Flower stood in front of the door, tail wagging, a sure sign that he knew and approved of the person on the other side. Lee stood on the porch, dressed this time in sweat shorts and a t-shirt that set off his muscles in a particularly attractive way. Kenzie felt herself perk up.

"Hi, Kenzie." Lee's smile faded as he took in her appearance. "Hey, I'm sorry, did I wake you?"

"Yeah." She scrubbed at her face, smearing soot over more of it. She made a solemn vow that she would never

ever collapse for a nap before showering again and wiped her face with her sleeve, transferring still more soot. Lee's grin reappeared, and she noticed that the corners of his eyes wrinkled in a particularly attractive way. Of course, she looked just wonderful, she groaned to herself. He would probably fade into the distance, and she would never see him again.

"I…uh… just got moved in, and I was wondering if you'd like to do a little pizza housewarming." His face was hopeful. Kenzie examined her hands, which were now dirty, trying not to grin.

"Sure. Let me go clean up. I'll come over in a few minutes. Which one?" Like she had not noticed the patrol car or even given him the address her very own self. Geez, Kenzie mentally kicked herself, think.

"Twenty fifteen." Lee gave her his heart-stopping smile, and Kenzie found herself come wide awake. "Come on over when you are ready…. See you." His voice trailed away as she grinned at him and shut the door. Kenzie raced up the stairs two at a time, skidding into the bathroom, all the time stripping out of her dirty clothes and then into the shower. Hormones could be genuinely wonderful things. In twenty minutes, she was ready, Flower was fed, and they were heading out the door.

Lee let her in at her first knock, and she went into a room the twin to hers. He had already set up his stereo, TV, and couch, Kenzie noted with a smile, even if everything else was still in boxes.

"You go everywhere with your dog?" Lee asked as he petted Flower.

"Pretty much. We're a package deal." Better warn him ahead of time. Lee's tolerance for Flower could dictate their entire potential relationship. "Hanging out with him has its benefits.

He gets to go places I don't, like first class on airplanes. And everyone fusses over him, so I meet a lot of interesting people. Do you mind?" Kenzie asked a little anxiously.

"No problem. I like dogs; I just don't have one. With my crazy schedule, it wouldn't be fair to the dog. I like cats, too." He looked a little sad at that.

"Yeah. If this pup was a civilian dog, I'd have the same problem" Kenzie looked around. "Looks nice. When'd you move in?"

"Last night. Thanks for the tip about it being vacant. Ummm... What do you like on your pizza?"

"Anything. Well, except onions and sausage. And anchovies, of course." She shuddered.

"How about Canadian bacon and pineapple?"

"My favorite."

"Mine, too." Lee placed the order, and as they waited for the pizza, each took stock of the other.

"How'd you end up in the fire service?" Lee asked.

"Same way you ended up a deputy. My dad was a firefighter, and my mom was a dispatcher. My whole family's in the emergency services."

"How many brothers and sisters do you have?"

"One of each. Sister's an ER doctor, brother's a wildland fire specialist, which is a fancy way of saying he jumps out of helicopters. I'm right in the middle." Kenzie grimaced. "You're an only child. Must have been lonely."

"Wasn't too bad. I've broken up my share of sibling fights, so I'm not sure I missed anything. Plus, my dad has been bringing home students for his entire career, so there were always college kids around. And, I was in every sport known to man, and the teams made my house their headquarters. I think Mom's cooking was mostly responsible for that, though." A ripple of laughter ran through his voice at some associated memory. He had a beautiful voice and used it almost professionally. Kenzie could imagine him as an audiobook reader or cartoon voice. "So, you, what, started on the engine?"

"Yeah." She looked down at her hands, remembering all the hard times and how much determination it had taken to stay on the engine when none of her rookie class or station mates wanted her. "On the engine, then I got my Criminal Justice degrees and went into fire investigation in my spare time." They exchanged wry looks, each knowing how little spare time either profession enjoyed. "Your dad was the best professor I had."

"And you were his star pupil. I've been hearing about you for years." Lee returned the compliment. Kenzie shrugged, embarrassed.

"Worried about your folks?" She changed the subject.

"Yeah. But I wanted to come back to a smaller town. My last post was as a deputy sheriff in Bear River County." He named the state capital's county. "It was all drugs, gangs, and prostitutes." Bear River County was mostly urban, and the sheriff's office was more of a city police department than a rural department.

"As opposed to here? Drugs, accidents, and loose livestock?" As a college town, they had their share of city problems, and with an interstate running around the edges of town, drugs were a huge problem.

"The loose livestock is a nice change," Lee admitted ruefully.

"You like being a cop?"

"Usually. I'm not planning on following in Dad's footsteps unless I teach at P.O.S.T." The doorbell rang, interrupting their conversation. Lee went to answer the door and came back with the pizza.

"So, there are five stations now?" Lee asked.

"Yep. I'm at Station One. We're attached to city hall, and we cover downtown and the university. Station Two handles the area east of the tracks. Station Three runs the western part and the county west of the interstate. Station Four covers the new subdivisions south of town, and Station Five is at the airport and covers the rest of the county. If you see three and five, you're lucky."

"They good?"

Kenzie snorted. "No, the old smoke eaters and the incorrigibles are stationed out there where they can't do too much damage. You'll be lucky if they show up, but don't quote me on that. The chief puts most of them at the airport because there aren't many calls. You know you're on his hit list when you get stationed out there. We back up four, but there are so many new houses that the fire rates are low. New construction and better adherence to fire codes."

"I'll keep that in mind. Are you planning to test for Lieutenant?"

"I don't know. Sometimes, I'm starting to feel my age on the fire line, and it's a young person's profession. But John and I.... We swore we'd always be partners. John's a real fire eater, and he'll never test for Lieutenant. So, I haven't tested either." Kenzie said thoughtfully. Lee sat back with a reserved look on his face.

"Who's John? Your boyfriend?" He asked. Kenzie laughed at the thought.

"Nope. Wouldn't be here if he was. John is John Barstow. He's my best friend, I guess. We've been partners for more than ten years now, him on the nozzle and me backing him up. I can't imagine fighting fires without him. But no, never my boyfriend."

"I see. Want another piece of pizza?" Lee offered the box to her with a smile. They sat and ate, conversation flowing smoothly. Kenzie enjoyed herself. Lee was pretty much perfect, his sense of humor dovetailed with hers, and he was easy on the eyes. When even his presence and her hormones could not keep her eyes from drifting shut, Lee walked her the few doors down to her house. He left her at the door with a pleasant good night and walked away with his hands in his pockets. Kenzie considered banging her head a few times against the door frame in frustration but decided against it. Exciting dreams were waiting, and a headache wouldn't help.

In the pale, crisp light of the next morning, they waved goodbye to each other as she left for the fire station where she was covering a shift for a sick firefighter, and he for the city streets.

Chapter 4

The next week, Kenzie's duty day fell on a Cub Scout Saturday. Herds of little boys with big eyes accompanied by harried parents trying to fill a meeting day with activities their little charges would find interesting. They were accompanied by freelance photographer Gordo Ellis.

"Hey, Gordo." Kenzie greeted him. He was a lot weird, but he was very good at his profession. "What're you doing here?"

"The paper wants a few warm and fuzzies. Counter-balance all the burning cars we've been publishing."

"Fire sells."

"Gloom doesn't, and that's what the fires have become. Warm and fuzzies, now, parents buy copies like hotcakes to send to grandma and all the aunts and uncles."

"You should get lots of wide-eyed cute kids shots today, then." She watched as he snapped off a few frames and collected names. He sauntered back, checking his shots on his view screen.

"Would you like copies of some of the shots and footage I've gotten from the arson fires?" His voice was casual. Kenzie studied the narrow features under the shaggy black hair pulled back into a ponytail. The arson investigator in her rose to the surface.

"Of course. I really like your work. But what about the paper and its policy? And doesn't that go against your policy of not helping law enforcement? You were pretty vehement about that in college."

Gordo shrugged. "Times change. And I'm technically a freelancer for both video and photographs. That way, they don't have to pay for insurance. I don't think about you as law enforcement, anyway."

"Gee, thanks, Gordo. You always know how to make a girl feel good." Kenzie tried not to snarl. She was very tired of that attitude. "I have to go rescue Flower." She shook her head as she walked away. Gordo was such a twit. She went to where Flower sat like an ebony statue, enduring the pats and pawings of a dozen little Cub Scouts. They flooded her with questions, which she answered with great patience.

"No, he's a Labrador Retriever, and he is a working member of the Fire Department," Kenzie explained. "Flower is an accelerant detection dog. An accelerant makes a fire start faster, burn hotter, or spread the fire, so it causes more damage.If something catches fire, Flower and I investigate the fire and look for things like gasoline that might have been used to start the fire. It's illegal and very dangerous to start fires. Flower can find clues that people might miss because his nose is so sensitive and well trained." She fielded the questions with a sense of humor.

Yes, he would play with people, but he had a critical job and was extremely focused on it. Yes, they trained every day on finding chemicals commonly used to start fires. No, he did not get a paycheck, but he got to fly first class, and therefore, so did she, and he could go anywhere she wanted to take him.

No, he wasn't a police dog. He was more like a detective. He wouldn't chase down bad guys and bite them. Yes, she had to go to school to learn to work with him. Flower gave a big sigh. He had heard it all before. Two of Kenzie's fellow firefighters rescued her from the Cubs' attention with the help of the big red fire truck.

"Three more packs," JohnB muttered as she walked past. Kenzie rolled her eyes and disappeared into the engine crew bedroom hallway. Each firefighter had his or her own tiny room, a change from the communal bedrooms of the old, pre-female fire stations. At least Flower rarely snored, which could not be said for the rest of her station mates.

A week later, Kenzie drove out into the county to investigate a trailer explosion. She had heard about this one on the department grapevine, and the fire marshal had told her to do her best. It had been a spectacular explosion with little left to put out, except a few trees that had been set on fire. Flower probably would not be needed; it would depend on what she found. This far out in the county, the explosion could have been caused by a couple factors. At the top of the list was a meth lab or a malfunctioning propane tank. Or both. Rural trailers and meth seemed to go together. She would have to be especially vigilant not to let Flower get hurt.

Kenzie stared in amazement at the damage. Trailers burned like an oil-soaked rag and usually were goners whether or not the fire department was Johnny-on-the-spot. Being this rural, it was hard to get fire coverage, and Station Five had had a devil of a time finding this off-grid location. It had been a clearing with the trailer backed against the side she was parked at. Several trees had been sheared off to her right.

A large pigsty was set at the farther end of the clearing, almost directly across the dirt road. To the far left was a shed that had been badly damaged in the fire. The trailer was a total loss, marked by a few charred pipes sticking up out of the ground, and the guts spread from the trailer to the farthest edge of the clearing. Insulation festooned the trees, and pieces of sheet metal siding littered the ground. The intensity of the blast had cleared any trash or belongings, but from the twisted frames, there had been piles of metal around the trailer – maybe bed frames and something that looked like an old tractor. Flower was definitely not getting out on this one.

Kenzie pulled her attention away from the fire ground and to the three men who waited for her. She sniffed as she got out of her SUV. The smell of pig was almost strong enough to overcome the stench of the burnt trailer.

Two brown and tans and one white police car were parked near the burned down trailer, the three drivers standing around, arms crossed and from the look of it, trading shop talk. Usually, there were not that many people who needed to watch the ruins. With a sudden lift of her heart, she recognized Lee, looking extra broad and muscular in his bulletproof vest. He turned and lifted his chin in hyper-masculine greeting, and she returned it with a smile. The three law officers walked over to her as she buckled on the fanny pack holding Flower's training aids. Kenzie nodded at them.

"Whatcha got?" Kenzie asked.

"Fire was reported at 2 a.m. last night and," one of the deputies glanced down at his clipboard, "uh, Station Five responded at 2:20 am, and they managed to save the foundation." Fire station humor. Kenzie gave him a mildly dirty look. It was one thing for firefighters to joke about shortcomings within the department, but not for outsiders. She turned and looked at the devastation, then slowly turned back.

"Given how rural this is, I'd say Station Five did a good stop. Not to mention, this place is not on any map." She reset her ball cap into a slightly more aggressive tilt.

"Er... yeah. Station Five put out what was left and then left the investigation to the fire marshal and you." He handed the rough report to Kenzie, who glanced at it, groaning inwardly at the handwriting and spelling. Sometimes she swore law enforcement scribbled on purpose.

"What are you doing here, Lee? Kind of far outside the city limits," she glanced at him.

"Slumming." He grinned at the other deputies. "We were at Post together. Plus, this is official police business." He drew himself up with a raised eyebrow. "I am the official meth lab specialist, having passed the USDA's Meth Lab 1010 class, which has not made it here yet."

"Cool. Meth lab?"

"Doesn't look like it. Probably survivalist. Watch for ammo." Well, that figured. Along with meth, rural trailers attracted the off-the-grid, anti-government weirdos. "Oh, and there's a class A still, down the path off to the south, past the pigs." he gestured toward the curious occupants of the sty who were peering through the wire and wood of their sty.

"Great. Any contact with the owner?"

"Not a word. We're looking for his vehicle, but who knows. At some heavily armed retreat in the hills, probably," one of the deputies answered.

"As long as he doesn't come home and take exception to me being here and his house being gone, I guess we'll be ok." Kenzie looked around the clearing and sighed. Do her best.

That was going to be a challenge. At least there were no dogs. "Well, shoot. This is going to take all day. I'd better get started." Kenzie made no move to walk away from Lee. The two deputies looked at each other with raised eyebrows.

"Yeah, Kenzie, you better get started," one said with a small grin. The other batted his eyes at her. Kenzie wrinkled her nose at him.

"I do believe we are interrupting a budding romance, Eddie. Fire service and police department. Guns and hoses. Now, that's a mental picture. How romantic," one said in a clinical voice. Kenzie felt her face grow hot and dropped her eyes, not daring to look at Lee. "I think Kenzie would like us to drop off the face of the earth."

"Yeah, yeah, go tell it to the papers. You still here, anyway?" Kenzie mock-growled at him.

"Come on, Eddie. We have work to do," he emphasized the word work. "You need us for anything...ah... not fire-related?"

"No. You'll get my report," Kenzie replied primly. The two deputies grinned at her and walked away, one of them holding his hands clasped together beside his cheek and beaming at the other in a rude mockery of Kenzie.

"Ah, my brother law enforcement officers. Gotta love them," Lee sighed.

"That was awkward," Kenzie grimaced.

"No doubt." He glanced at his fellow law enforcement buddies to see how far away they were. "I've been trying to run into you for a week, now."

"I do have a phone. Several of them. And I live next door to you, practically."

"I know."

"And the fire station is right next to the police station."

"Like I'm going to walk into the fire station. You think my brothers in blue are bad? I can just imagine all those firefighters, gossiping like a bunch of old ladies." He sang a measure from the Music Man, the gossiping old lady song. His voice was really very good, Kenzie noted with surprise. "Not to mention glaring at me like eight big brothers and fathers," Lee shuddered and grinned. "Unlike these prurient bozos." He gestured at his friends, who were watching them over their car doors with avid interest. They returned the gesture with interest, laughter drifting over to where Kenzie and Lee stood. "Can I see you tonight for dinner?" He asked quietly. Kenzie felt an insuppressible grin growing.

"I'd like that."

"See you when you get home. I'm covering for someone, but I'll be off at five."

"I'll probably be back about then. How about six? Gives me a chance to clean up," Kenzie suggested. He gave her another of his heart-stopping smiles and walked toward his car.

Kenzie loved the grace with which he moved. Being in a physically demanding profession made her appreciate an athlete. Both the fire service and law enforcement could pack on the pounds over the years as stress alternating with boredom took its toll. Lee had managed to avoid that trap quite nicely, so far.

Lee waved and drove away. The other two deputies, with whom she had worked for years, stayed hanging over their car doors, gossiping. Kenzie groaned to herself. Law enforcement was almost as bad as firefighters for gossip. There was no doubt this would be all over the sheriff's department by noon, the police station by three, and then the fire department by evening. Then the teasing would really start. The first thing rookies were told at fire school was if they could not take teasing, the fire service had no room for them.

"Bye bye, boys. I gotta get to work." She wiggled her fingers at them and turned away. She could hear them joshing each other but did not really want to know exactly what they were saying. She finally heard the car engines start, and the two deputies drove off.

Before she let Flower loose, she began by walking around the remains of the house trailer. Explosion and fire in some order- either the propane tank had gone up, or the trailer had caught fire, and the tank had bleve-d as the boiling propane rapidly expanded. She sniffed but only smelled burned house trailer and pig. Kenzie grinned to herself. That was why Flower was on board. The requisite redwood deck was blown off to one side, splintered beyond repair with char marks from fire blown out by the explosion. This would be Wall A; Kenzie made a few notes and snapped several photos.

The middle of the trailer had blown out away from the propane tank and across the grassy clearing. Some of it had gone towards the sty, and at least one of the boards holding them in was broken. Kenzie picked her way across the litter, thankful for heavy work boots. She turned over a few of the largest pieces she could identify as either roof or wall. The interiors were clean, and any burn marks were on the surfaces that had landed up.

The bedroom end of the trailer was relatively undamaged. It had been the furthest away from the tank. Undamaged was perhaps not the correct term. It was filled with garbage belongings. The stench was hideous. Hoarder. She recognized the symptoms from too many houses declared off-limits after they had gone in for a rescue. There seemed to be a few dogs missing as well since there was the definite presence of dog crap all over.

She worked her way around to the rear of the trailer. This side had absorbed most of the blast, and there was not much left. Kenzie documented it all, including the propane tank that had peeled open like a banana. The walls closest to the tank had caught fire and were mostly gone. It appeared to be the kitchen, although that was a guess from having been in a fair number of trailers over the years. She finished her tour around the trailer and thought for a few moments.

Kenzie walked a grid pattern out from the trailer, documenting where everything had landed, including the pressure valve located on a piece of metal hanging from a tree. She would need a look at that, but it would require a crane or a powerful wind.

Why survivalists never went solar was beyond her. That way, they could be truly off the grid, instead of requiring occasional visits by the propane man. Probably too liberal and granola for their tastes.

Once she had a map of the remains of the propane tank documented, she went back and took more photos. Digital images were cheap. Screwing up a case because of lack of documentation – now that was expensive. She checked what was left of every appliance she could find. Most had been destroyed by the blast and not one had been on.

Time for the fire dog. Kenzie went back to her SUV to get Flower. She fished four booties out of her SUV and shook them out for good measure. Flower was too valuable to risk severe pad cuts or burns through her carelessness. She put booties on Flower's feet and let him out of the SUV, noting sadly that he moved stiffly for the first few steps before going into work mode made him forget being an older dog.

Walking beside him, she directed his head and nose down, letting the super-sensitive nose do its work. He hit on nothing, confirming her suspicions. She suspected that the tank had bleve-d, a boiling liquid expanding vapor explosion, that the pressure valve should have prevented. The whys it had bleve-d would have to wait until the value could be examined.

The pigs grunting caught her attention. There seemed to be a lot going on in the sty. Curious, Kenzie walked over. One of the railings at the top of the fence was broken inward, and she examined it carefully. The break was fresh. Pigs were one of the animals she had not had much experience with, but she would guess they were hungry or thirsty from the squeals and grunts. Depending on how long the owner had been gone... the tank was dry. Kenzie located a hose and turned on the well pump. Give them water now and call animal control for a welfare check.

Once the pigs had finished drinking, Kenzie watched them for a few more minutes. Once she was used to the stench, they were sort of interesting. One of the big ones was wallowing down into the mud, sinking its nose deep into the sludge and turning it over. It snuffled closer at some random piece of trash and flipped it out of the muck. Kenzie froze, her brain suddenly identifying the refuse as a dental partial. She raised her eyes across the pigsty, past the broken board, and up to the trailer. A running man knowing the propane tank was going to blow might come this way. She should pick up the partial. As she put one hand on the top of the fence, the biggest pig clattered its teeth, and the little piggie eyes were no longer friendly. Pictures would suffice for this suspicion.

She had always heard that a pig would eat anything that fell into its sty. Pork was definitely off the menu.

A still, Lee had said. Kenzie had never seen one. May as

well haul herself down there and take a look. It might prove educational. Calling Flower to her, she set off down the well-worn path about 100 yards. The still looked pretty much like all the cartoons she had seen of them. The smell of Everclear grade shine made her nose itch. You would have to be crazy to drink this brew. Kenzie headed back up the trail, stopping when Flower stared off into the weeds. He whined and sat down. Kenzie peered at the little-used trail, so faint that it was practically not there. All sorts of possibilities occurred to her, from dead bodies to a booby-trapped trail to a marijuana field. Cautiously, she moved onto the underused trail, checking her steps to ensure no unpleasant surprises were hidden there. It led, disappointingly but not surprisingly, to the midden heap.

Cans, bottles, copper tubing, and paper trash were piled haphazardly in a small hollow. The two fur rugs were an interesting addition. Her brain slowly made sense of what she was seeing. Not rugs, but dogs. Very dead dogs shot through the head. Kenzie suddenly became uncomfortably aware that the woods had fallen silent. Nothing chirped or moved. She moved her hand to smooth down the hair on the back of her neck, adrenaline coursing through her system. She was very alone out here. Kenzie turned and headed back to Flower. She was unreasonably grateful to see the dog waiting patiently. If this had been the horror movie, it felt like Flower would have been dead or gone.

Kenzie hustled down the path, trying not to scuttle, in case anyone was watching, but definitely hurrying, happy to see her SUV, like Flower, still in one piece. She loaded Flower and jumped in herself, locking the doors with a quick push. It even started on the first try, hallelujah. The banjo music that had swirled through her head on the way back to the truck faded away. Keeping a careful watch out the windows in the rear-view mirror, Kenzie waited until the adrenaline had slowed to a manageable trickle. She called the sheriff, who dispatched someone, hopefully not the odious Eddie, to take a closer look.

Kenzie was happy to see the deputy's car nose down the road. She was still a bit freaked out and glad to be heading back to town. Each mile made her feel better and, oddly, more tired as she relaxed. As much as she was looking forward to going out with Lee, all she really wanted to do was crawl home to her comfy couch and sit in her nice safe living room. A preemptive dinner selection would then be in order.

Kenzie made a stop at her favorite Thai restaurant on the way home, a small hole in the wall with amazing food and no low health inspections. It was probably a bad sign, she reflected, when they knew exactly what she was going to order, but tonight something vegetarian for her, the memory of the pigs and the dental partial and the dead dogs leaving a bad taste in her mouth.

Lee could have the curry dish she usually loved. She chatted with the owners and then hurried home to put dinner in the oven. By the time she was home, her stomach had recovered enough to do happy little drops of excitement. Almost five o'clock. Time to hurry. A quick shower, and she would be ready for anything. Amazing how hormones or quite possibly lust could reenergize even the most tired person.

When the doorbell rang, she opened the door to a bouquet of balloons held by a hand that thrust them out to her.

"Happy June 30th," Lee said from behind the balloons. Kenzie took them with a laugh.

"This is...umm... unexpected. Thank you. I guess I don't have to stick them in water."

"Probably not a good idea. Something smells wonderful."

"Come on in. I ordered out Thai. I hope you like it."

"I'm sure I will. I wasn't expecting you to provide dinner. I was going to take you out." Lee took the hand that was not holding the balloons. Kenzie blushed.

"Oh. I had a hell of a day, and I'd really like to stay home if you don't mind. I think the pigs either ate the property owner or his killer. And I found his dogs on the trash heap out near the still." She offered. Lee grimaced. Kenzie stepped back, and he followed her into the house, still holding her hand.

"The pigs? Ate someone?"

"Unless they wear dentures."

"Good lord. What was up with the dogs?"

"Shot dead. That was severely disgusting. I ordered vegetarian for myself. No meat for a while."

"You poor thing." Lee pulled Kenzie into a gentle hug. Kenzie put her arms around him, reveling in the feel of muscle under her hands. It had been a very long time since her last relationship, one that had dissolved into jealousy over her profession. Much to her disappointment, the hug stayed chaste.

"Your Thai dinner smells too good to pass up. How about a rain check on the going out?" Lee said kindly. Kenzie looked into his eyes and was lost. His smile made her toes curl. Flower came into the room, and the dog's tail thudded gently against the wall. It was nice, Kenzie thought, that her partner and roommate approved of this potential companion.

The meal was wonderful, the company divine, and he left without kissing her good night or even another hug. Kenzie sighed in frustration. He could not be married. The James's would never have played matchmaker if that was the case. He certainly seemed to like her, but, but, but... her brain sputtered. Cold shower and some arson manuals ought to about round out her evening. Glumly, she headed up to her room and some heavy reading.

In the morning, Kenzie finished her initial report and worked with Flower. Her phone remained annoyingly quiet just when she could use a good fire to investigate. Never failed. But she could take a closer look at something that had been bothering her—the car arsonist.

After a couple of months, the car arsonist was still going strong. Kenzie plotted the fires on a big city map pinned to her wall. There had to be some connecting factor, but no interviews had turned up a common enemy so far. There wasn't even a pattern to the burns. It seemed completely random, but Kenzie knew somewhere there was a clue.

Arsonists were only random on the surface. Underneath, they followed a pattern as clearly as she would a road map. The Bureau of Alcohol, Tobacco, and Firearms had spent a considerable amount of time and money profiling arsonists, who tended to be male. In general, women set fires to their ex-lover's belongings or, in rare instances, their own homes, usually for attention or revenge, occasionally as a means to murder. Men were more universal in their destruction and in their motives.

Word had been sent out to doctors, clinics, and hospitals to alert for suspicious burns. Many arson fires were solved when the arsonist was arrested after being admitted to the hospital for serious burns. Since arson was a crime, doctors had to report suspicious burns, just as they were required to report gunshot or stab wounds.

Arsonists fell into four basic categories. The youthful ones, motivated by excitement or the need to vandalize something, comprised one group. Those who felt they had been wronged by society made up the next group. Revenge for perceived injustices or fires for profit were their motivations. People with political objectives, the extremists on society's fringes, or those wanting to conceal crimes were the third group. Throughout history, this group had been so prevalent that they had even given name to a particular form of an incendiary device, the Molotov Cocktail.

But by far, the most destructive were the serial arsonists. These men set fires repeatedly for a sense of power and control, a need set so deeply within them that they could not control it. They could bring out the fire department in full force whenever they wanted. They could spread panic and fear. The ATF had a profile for these people. Kenzie pulled out the sheet and reviewed it. Nothing jumped out at her, screaming, "it's me." She made a face in frustration.

People had three different lives; Kenzie reminded herself. The home life, the social life, and the secret life. These were kept separate from each other in varying degrees, and it was the secret life that caused the problems. Only one person knew those secret desires and dreams that fueled the inner vision of him or herself. The outlet for the secret life was usually harmless- books, movies, white lies. But sometimes, the outlet took a destructive turn, resulting in drug use, arson, and murder.

The arsonist was clearly in the fourth group. But the who and why evaded her. A fool's circle. If she could answer one of the questions, she would know the answer to the rest. She picked up one of Flower's tennis balls and threw it against the map, narrowly missing the pins designating last week's fires, right on the city's edge. The tennis ball made a squelching noise and left a circle of doggy slobber. Kenzie swore and stomped out to find paper towels. Lee should be home. Last night he had said he was working days, so home and awake was a definite possibility. Maybe he would be interested in a bike ride.

Kenzie wheeled her bike out of the storage shed in the back yard and threaded it through the gate at the side of her townhouse. Backyard access was a benefit to living, in the end-most townhome, that and more windows. Flower watched with a sigh through the front window and then flopped down. He never got to go on bike rides, and he greeted the bike with grim resignation. He was too valuable to risk taking on a bike ride, and Kenzie was hesitant to let him go on runs with her because, although he had a clean bill of health, he was still a Labrador. Hips were always a potential problem.

Kenzie wheeled her bike down to Lee's house and knocked on the door. It swung open almost immediately. Lee looked at her unsmilingly with a law enforcement flat gaze. He was dressed in skintight black pants and a tight white t-shirt, a black jacket draped over his gym bag. His hair was spiked into an 80's style 'do. Kenzie's eyebrows climbed up to new heights at the picture he presented.

"Um, hi." Kenzie was a bit unnerved by the unwelcome in his very stance. "I was going out for a bike ride and thought you might like to come along."

"I can't. I have somewhere to go. Every Wednesday and every Saturday. And I'll be late if I don't leave soon."

"Ah. Well, then. I guess I'll see you around." Kenzie turned her bike around and got on. Lee said nothing as she locked her feet into the pedals and rode away. Embarrassment threaded its way through her guts and up to her face. She felt hot and sweaty and felt like hiding from him. Maybe she had seriously misread him. Kenzie glanced back. Lee was slamming the topper door shut on his truck. Kenzie shook her head. Fine. And more than fine. He could bloody well come to her from now on. A few minutes later, Lee's truck whizzed past her. At least, he gave a hint of a wave. Kenzie glared after the truck. Fine, fine, fine.

Chapter 5

The next evening, Kenzie laid on her station bed, reading a book. They had had a long morning of training and an afternoon of inspections. The front door buzzer sounded, and she put down her book. It usually signified someone needing blood pressure checks or other simple medical care, and she was not feeling up to answering the door today and being polite to whoever it was. Someone else could rack up the patient contact hours. She went back to her book and managed to get a page read before commotion drifted in from the day room. Something out of the ordinary, and she perked up her ears, waiting to hear if she needed to help the medics or if the doorbell was something worth getting up for.

"Oooh, John. Isn't that special." A deep voice cooed in a shaky falsetto.

"They aren't for me, you dope." JohnB shot back. "They're for Kenzie."

"Aww."

"Our Kenzie?" Tones of disbelief. Kenzie sat up; ears metaphorically pricked.

"Looky here, Kenzie." JohnB peeked into her room. "Flowers for you. Someone must think you're a girl." JohnB held out a vase of mixed flowers, mostly reds, and pinks with a blue stem of something thrown in for good measure, lots of little white flowers that Kenzie knew from experience would dry out and crumble everywhere.

"Cool."   Kenzie rolled up off her bed, the book falling unheeded to the floor. She went to take them, but JohnB. held them out of her reach.

"Spill the beans, Kenz. Who thinks you're a girl?"

"Don't be an idiot, JB. Give me the flowers."

"Tell first." JohnB looked down at her. His blue eyes twinkled with good humor.

"Give. Me. The. Flowers. Stinky." Kenzie gritted her teeth. JohnB blinked at her in surprise. Kenzie was usually great at taking jokes. He handed her the vase. Kenzie could feel the cool radiating off the flowers and smell the chilled fragrance of hothouse flowers.

"Who are they from?" JohnB asked.

"I don't know." Kenzie opened the card and pulled it out. "Friday night, 6:30, dinner." No signature. But then there wasn't one needed. A grin began to creep out.

"Who is it?" John teased.

"Secret admirer. See, it's not signed." Kenzie flashed the card at him. She could not help the grin.

"I have four sisters, Kenzie, tell me another one. Who's the mystery man?"

"None of your business, Stinky."

"Come on, tell your big brother firefighter." John batted his eyes at her."Who is it?" Kenzie shook her head. "OK. Firefighter? Nope. Not one of them would dare. So, someone you just met. Okay. At an investigation? Nope. Suspects are bad boyfriends. Another dog handler? Nope. Let's see. You don't have any life outside the fire service, so…"

"I do so have a life," Kenzie replied, stung. "I must, or I wouldn't be getting flowers. God knows you'd never send anyone flowers." She put her nose in the air and winked at her best friend.

"That is because I am a catch in my own right. One date with me, and I never need to send flowers." JohnB retorted. Kenzie snorted.

"You're just going to have to suffer without knowing. Go away. I want to be alone with my flowers." She touched the petals of one flower gently.

"He nice?" JohnB. asked, suddenly serious. Kenzie looked up and smiled.

"Yeah, Stinky. He's real nice." Her voice went soft. John nodded once and tapped on the wall.

"Good." He went out, and Kenzie stared absently out the door after him. JohnB was her partner and oldest friend in the fire service. But that had not always been the case. In rookie school, John had been one of the instructors and her tormentor, always pushing, teasing, tripping, and making her life a living hell. If something went wrong, he was there to criticize and not in a nice way, complete with teaching, but in a nasty way, meant to humiliate her. He had been the instigator of all the pranks. Kenzie had known what to expect, thanks to her father's lifetime in the fire service, so she had not given up, but it had been spirit-crushing.

When she had qualified as Firefighter I, despite JohnB's best efforts to trip her up or make her so miserable that she would washout, the powers that be, in a burst of sadism, had stationed them together. Kenzie had always wondered if there had not been a hope in the upper echelons that she would fail and that JohnB's torture had been condoned. He had certainly never been reprimanded for it. She had never complained, that would have been fatal to her career, but the pressure had been unbelievably awful. Only her parents' support and faith in her abilities had kept her going.

Women in the fire service were often viewed with suspicion by firefighter wives because female firefighters lived for twenty-four hours out of every seventy-two with men who were someone else's husbands. They were viewed with suspicion by male firefighters who considered women as physically weak and inept. Some departments had hired anything female in a rush to avoid sanctions by the federal government. Many of the women had not worked out.

She had heard of big-city stations hiring anything with two X chromosomes, only to find that most of them were not qualified and most definitely not suited to firehouse life. One not so old firefighter had told her it was her fault he found her physically attractive and could not keep his mind and other body parts focused on the job at hand when she was around.

Other male firefighters were worried that a woman's lack of physical strength would put them in danger. It was a constant challenge to maintain physical training and upper body strength, and Kenzie felt by using her brains, she could work smarter and thus equal out the differences. The fire service was no longer about just brawn; brains counted as well.

For Kenzie, who had grown up with firefighting, the tools of the fire service were familiar. For many other women not used to mechanic work or home improvement, fire service tools could be baffling. Kenzie had read studies that indicated when departments took a little extra time and effort to teach rookie women (and some men) about the tools, aptitude increased exponentially. For every woman who succeeded, there were two or more who failed, and each failure made it that much harder on the next woman. For some reason, the successes never seemed to rub off on the next woman.

At any rate, JohnB's torture had been carefully planned, but Kenzie stuck it out, refusing to take legal action until she had tried everything else. And then miracles had happened, two in fact. One had been silly, a call gone wrong, with no dire consequences, just a lot of sweating. But the other had been moments of sheer terror for both her and John. It had been during this second event that John had decided she could indeed haul his butt out of a burning building and that maybe she deserved a chance. They had been on a statewide training, and JohnB had been the nozzleman with two others from another county. In their training, firefighters went forward onto their knees. In the other firefighters' case, they had been trained to sit back.

When they had advanced on the fire, JohnB had knelt forward, the other two sat back, and the weight shift had slammed the nozzle into JohnB's face, knocking his helmet awry and smashing his face mask off-center. Kenzie had been next to them on another hose line. She had turned her hose on him, just as the intense heat from the fire had begun to scorch his face. Then, somehow, the two firefighters on each line had scooted up to hold the nozzles and hoses, and Kenzie had grabbed JohnB by the air pack and dragged him out of the building, the stream from one hose following them out. She had dropped him on the dirt and stood looking down at him through her mask. He had taken off his shattered mask, looking at it in dismay.

"Not bad for a rookie." He had said, his voice a little shaken.

"Even a girl rookie?" Kenzie pulled her mask off, looking at him with disdain. JohnB had flushed.

"Especially a girl rookie." From that moment on, his torment had lessened a bit, but it would not be until the Great Snake Fire that he became her greatest ally. Eventually, Kenzie had decided his change was genuine, and they had become best friends. She had bestowed his nickname of Stinky upon him, for reasons best forgotten. Her own nickname, Fire Chick, had been his derogatory name for her, now worn proudly on the back of her helmet.

Kenzie smiled briefly at the memory and then smelled the flowers, touching each cool bloom with a fingertip, and made a silent wish on each before going back to her reading. Her eyes kept drifting back to the flowers and her mind to pleasant daydreams. She turned the pages but could not have said what she had just read.

By six-thirty on Friday evening, Kenzie's room looked as if a dozen girls getting ready for prom had invaded it. Clothes were thrown in piles, shoes littered the floor, jewelry spilled out of the box on the dresser. Kenzie looked ruefully at herself in the mirror. Her clothing selection was a bit limited.

Clothing worn to an arson investigation was soon ruined by smoke residue and debris. Her off-hours were usually dedicated to working with Flower as his training had to be completed once a day, every day until he retired. Kenzie had managed to scrape together a skirt and blouse and the resolution to shop for a few nice outfits.

Lee knocked promptly on her door and was greeted by Flower, who fawned on him. Lee rubbed the dog's ears as he looked approvingly at Kenzie.

"I don't think I've ever seen you in a skirt before. You look nice."

"It's hard to fight fires in one of these." She made a face. "You look nice, too." His look was completely different from the tight outfit of the disastrous Wednesday. He wore an eye blindingly wild Hawaiian shirt and dark slacks, and his hair was soft. Kenzie considered running her fingers through it, but reserve held her hand back.

"Well, then. Now that our mutual admiration session is over, shall we go to dinner?" He offered her his elbow with a smile. Kenzie tucked her hand into the crook of his elbow, and they went out to Lee's truck. He opened her door and helped her tuck her skirt in. Lee was a calm driver, unlike some law enforcement types she had driven with. Sometimes, that career path resulted in severe lead foot-itis.

In the restaurant parking lot, Lee went around to open her door and help her out. Kenzie smiled up at him, thrilled by the courtesy he was showing, while at the same time, he recognized her as a professional in her own right. It was nice to be treated as something special on occasion, especially when she had to be so careful to never fail. Kenzie resumed her hand position. Excitement shivered through her as Lee covered her hand with his and smiled. Maybe he was just reserved and cautious and therefore slow in moving any relationship forward.

The restaurant was crowded, and Lee went to give his name for the waiting list.

"Should have thought to call..." Lee said softly to her. Over the hubbub of the crowd, a light, tinkling laugh rang out. Lee stopped, head going up like a hunting dog, searching the room. His eyes went flat, and his face lost all animation. Law enforcement mode, Kenzie recognized the mannerisms.

"What's the matter?"

"I... nothing." His face grew even sterner, and his voice dropped in pitch. He maneuvered her so that his back was to the crowd.

"Well, if it isn't Lee. Fancy meeting you here, sweetheart. And looking so good with your clothes on, for a change." Kenzie peered around him. The woman who stood behind Lee was her worst nightmare. Short, but managing to look tall and elegant. Perfectly coiffed hair is a shade of brown that gleamed and threw back the lights. As Lee turned to face the woman, Kenzie had the overwhelming desire to smooth down her wild curls. "And with such a... lovely companion." The woman's voice was measured and with perfect diction, sweet, but her eyes were cold.

Of course, she would have perfect makeup and clothes cut to show off every curve, Kenzie thought, whoever she was. The woman's eyes flicked over Kenzie's plain skirt and blouse, and she smiled contemptuously, mistaking Kenzie for a lightweight.

"Hello, Tina." Lee's voice was distant. He looked down his nose at the woman, who looked at him with an expression partly of hatred and partly of desire. Kenzie looked at Lee and felt her courage slip a little. She wanted to step back and hide from the scorn in the woman's face when her eyes had dismissed her, but then a nice bracing shot of adrenaline coursed through her system, and she moved perceptibly closer to Lee, slipping her arm around him. He might think he did not need the help, but this woman was bad news.

Lee responded by running a hand down her back to stop in a possessive curve on her waist. Kenzie was almost as tall as Lee, and together they made a formidable couple. Kenzie watched as the woman tried to figure out how to get closer to Lee. Kenzie stood her ground, letting her eyes travel down to the woman's shoes. Perfect except for the thick ankles, not very attractively set off by the shoes she wore. She gave a half-smile of derision, and the woman caught it, face flushing slightly, expression changing to irritation for a brief second. In a flash of woman-to-woman nonverbal communication, Kenzie had just staked her territory and challenged the newcomer.

"I heard you moved down here. I'm so glad I transferred here as well, to Channel 4, lead evening anchor. We have so much to talk about." The woman... purred, Kenzie decided, was the perfect term for her voice.

"I have nothing to say to you, Tina. If you'll excuse us..."

"Before you introduce me to your latest love? Why, how perfectly lovely to not worry about dressing up. The money you must save being a nature girl. Where do you have your hair done? I haven't seen curls like that since the Shirley Temple film-a-thon on PBS last year. You must tell me your hairdresser's name." Tina's voice was sweetness itself, but Kenzie bristled.

"They are natural. Unlike yourself, I see. Who is your plastic surgeon?" Kenzie could feel her teeth grating together. Gauntlets were thrown, blood drawn, pistols at ten paces, Kenzie thought. She waited for the battle to continue. She thought she felt Lee's stomach muscle quiver. If he laughed...

"Hey, Kenzie." Another man joined their tense circle.

"Gordon, I thought you were waiting on a table for us," Tina said sharply, not taking her eyes off Lee. Gordo flushed.

"They're calling it right now. I came to get you before we lose it."

"Hey, Gordo." Kenzie smiled tightly at her friend. He looked bewildered by the tension. He had always been an odd duck and not quite socially acceptable. Whatever was he doing with this thick-ankled fashion plate?

"Do introduce us, Gordon," Tina commanded.

"This is Kenzie Stevenson. We went to college together. She's a firefighter and has an arson dog." Gordo responded awkwardly. Tina's delicately and perfectly plucked eyebrows rose.

"Really, how interesting. I really must interview you." The nastiness was gone, replaced instantly with sweetness and light.

"I'm afraid you've been scooped on that story."

"That was my line, sweetie. You've got yesterday's news there under your jealous little hand." Tina responded with a malicious smirk in Lee's direction. With a triumphant smile, Tina tucked her hand into Gordo's elbow and escorted him away. Kenzie removed her hand, feeling a burn of embarrassment wrap itself around her spine. Lee recaptured her hand and held it tight. She could swear there was a slight tremor, but from just which part of that encounter, she could not guess.

"Who in the hell was that? And what was that all about?" Kenzie shook her head to clear it.

"Oh. Nobody important."

"Really. I've just exchanged insults with someone I've never met, and I don't know precisely why." Kenzie waited; eyebrows raised. Lee sighed.

"That, my dear, was my past. My ex-girlfriend, Tina Sarkasian, the gods' gift to television news."

"James, table for two?" The hostess called out.

"Do you want to stay, Kenzie?"

"I'm too angry to eat."

"Me, too, but to retreat now would be cowardly. C'mon. I'll

buy you something with lots of chocolate and caffeine in it. You'll feel better." Heads high, they followed the hostess to their table. After the flurry of ordering dinner was over, Kenzie lifted her eyebrows at Lee.

"So, tell me more."

"I'm breaking a major male taboo."

"What, kissing, and telling?"

"No. Discussing the evil ex-girlfriend with the hopefully new girlfriend." Lee assumed a somber expression. Kenzie rolled her eyes with a giggle. She took his hand across the table.

"You'll live. Tell all."

"Okay. Tina was my girlfriend, back in the City. She was a reporter for the Fox affiliate."

"Ah, balanced, sane, and fair. Why does that not surprise me? And she's the real reason you left."

"A good part of it, yes."

"So, why is she here?"

"At a guess, she's followed me here."

"Four's the ABC affiliate. Maybe they pay better." Kenzie felt a definite unease.

"No. Even as lead anchor, coming to work here is a step down the TV ladder. She had her own little cult following back in the city." Lee thought for a moment. "Tina's weird, really vindictive. I broke up with her because she was in love with the glamour of dating a law enforcement officer, but the reality annoyed her. And she took the reality out on me. That, and because something I told her in confidence, showed up on the news a few days later, with no other source I could ferret out. That was a real mess. When we split up, she took our cat and had it euthanized. Then she started making harassing phone calls to my sheriff." Lee spoke in clipped words. Kenzie mentally stumbled over the "our cat" phrase before catching up with the rest of what Lee was saying.

"Did you file a restraining order?"

"That would be like you starting a kitchen fire and having to call in the fire department." Their food arrived, and conversation stopped while they seasoned, cut, and took the first mouthful.

"How's yours?"

"Great. You?"

"I was hungrier than I thought. So, go on."

"There's nothing much left to tell. I left soon after that." They ate in silence for a while.

"How'd you know about the plastic surgeon?" He asked curiously.

"Oh, please. Us nature girls can always smell out the fakes. It's self-preservation." Her words were a little bitter. "Does my hair still really look like Shirley Temple's?" Kenzie pulled one springy strand straight and let go. It sprang back into a perfect corkscrew.

"Only in a superficial way." Lee tried to be diplomatic, but the comparison was inevitable.

"I suppose the crack about your clothes on meant the obvious?" Kenzie asked. Lee's face grew even more closed.

"I expect so. Let's not discuss her anymore. She's the past."

They watched as Tina and Gordo left the restaurant. Kenzie recognized the puppy love expression on Gordo's face and shook her head. She wasn't sure what Tina saw in the nerdy photographer, but it gave her an awful feeling. Gordo's conversation was limited to his shoots, and his hygiene was frequently questionable. Gordo's looks were not what would generally attract someone like Tina. Lee's expression was unreadable as his eyes followed them out.

It seemed for the next few weeks, everywhere Kenzie and Lee went, Tina was there, watching, making snide comments, or just being seen. Kenzie decided Tina had a sixth sense when it came to Lee's activities. Eventually, the appearances stopped, and Kenzie no longer saw Tina at every turn. She did, however, avoid watching Channel 4 news.

Fire had been his god, his muse. And now there was another. At first, he had been charmed, and then she had coiled around his heart like a snake. That is what he would call her, deep in his thoughts. She was like the snake in the garden of Eden. She had discovered the secret that was his alone, that he was the god of fire, and that fire answered his call. At first, the snake had done nothing with the knowledge of his addiction to fire and setting car fires had been enough. And then anger had swept through the snake, and he had been terrified.

The snake whispered in his ear, giving him ideas he had never entertained and making promises he had only dreamed of in his darkest, most private thoughts. He would have to follow the snake's teachings. And the snake promised that when Kenzie came to him, the snake would go away. He was very, very frightened of the snake. Only fire held the snake at bay.

Several days later, Kenzie was in her backyard, hiding rags in various places. The rags each had a drop of some sort of hydrocarbon accelerant on them, and Flower would have to find each. Training had to be done any day that there wasn't an investigation, and Kenzie varied her sessions as much as possible.

The day before, she had gone to a school after hours and

let Flower find accelerants in lockers and classrooms. Several teachers and the principal had joined in the training enthusiastically and had found creative places to hide the samples. Flower had found almost all of them. He had missed on a rarely used copier toner accelerant. Kenzie would be working with him on that particular one. Just then, her cell phone rang and she answered.

"'Lo?"

"Want to go for a bike ride?" Lee asked.

"I can't right now. I have to do a training session with Flower."

"Ah. Would it... can I watch?"

"Sure. Come on over. I'll wait for you."

"See you in a few minutes." Lee hung up. Kenzie pushed the phone's off button and slid it back in the holder.

Lee met them in the backyard, where Flower greeted him with a wagging tail. Kenzie let Lee scratch Flower's ears and then recalled the dog. Lee went to sit quietly on a garden chair, watching intently.

Kenzie started the training with a review of Flower's basic commands. These were simple obedience training work and served to focus Flower on his job at hand. Because Flower was a very high-profile dog, he had to have impeccable manners. Flower was rewarded with a combination of food and squeaky toy play. Kenzie kept special dog treats in her fanny pack, and after each successful command, she slipped him a treat. Once they started work on accelerants, the squeaky toy came into play. Flower watched her intently, tail gently waving. He loved his work, and she was careful to make it fun. Nothing ruined a dog like making work a slog.

She guided Flower around the yard, giving Flower the command to seek. Almost immediately, Flower's sensitive nose caught the scent, and he veered toward a garden gnome and sat down. He pointed his nose directly at the gnome with paws on either side of the gnome and waited. Kenzie slipped him a treat.

"Show me better," Kenzie asked quietly. Flower dropped his nose down and nudged at the gnome. "Good dog." She slipped him another treat and turned the gnome over. A small piece of rag with a single drop of gasoline was under it. They moved on to the next section of the yard. Kenzie knew the scent she wanted to train him on was very near, and so she kept guiding his nose past the "plant." When the dog finally sat and pointed, she fed him a treat and then pulled out the special squeaky toy. She squeaked it vigorously and threw it for Flower, praising him each time he returned it.

After a few minutes, they went on to the next sample, another drop of copier toner. Flower found it without fail and went on to locate all the other samples. After the training session, Kenzie released him from work mode, and Flower brought a tennis ball to her.

Kenzie took the ball over to Lee and threw it. She sat down next to Lee, and Flower brought the ball back. The two humans took turns throwing the ball for the dog, who never tired of chasing it.

"That was really interesting," Lee said. "I've watched them work the K-9s at POST and thought it looked like fun."

"I love it. Did you ever think of working with dogs?"

"No. That pretty much required military training, and I wasn't interested in the service. I went straight into law enforcement as soon as I was old enough to be on the campus parking enforcement squad. Law enforcement's all I ever wanted to do."

"No." Kenzie laughed. "Tell me you weren't one of them. I hated the parking police. I swear they knew my car. I finally gave up driving and rode my bike to school, uphill both ways in knee-deep snow."

"Yep. Orange vest and all. It was great training, talking jocks and occasionally jockettes out of beating the snot out of me when I ticketed their cars."

"I'll bet. Why didn't you go to school here?"

"I wanted to be far away from here. Plus, the idea of my dad teaching me," Lee shuddered. "You think he was hard on you. I'd have been lucky to graduate."

"He's not that bad." Kenzie chided.

"Not for you, maybe. At any rate, it was time to leave. Just like it was time to come home. So, what were you doing with Flower today?" Lee changed the subject.

"We were training on a new scent. You notice it only took Flower's nose one hit to learn the smell."

"What was it?"

"Copier toner. Some of it's pretty flammable since it can be paraffin-based. People don't know about it, but crooks do, and some use it to cover up crimes in office buildings. So, we trained on it. He'll never miss again."

"Does he always learn so quickly?"

"In the beginning, it was slow. Flower was too rambunctious, but the minute he figured out this weird human game, he's been unstoppable."

"How'd you get him?"

"I applied for training with the ATF. They have a training center in Connecticut, and they start the dogs. We came in later and learned how to handle them and to keep up the training.

We have to go back each year for recertification, but Flower is so busy he doesn't have time to forget any training."

"Where'd they get him?"

"Would you believe he was a guide dog reject? I still keep in contact with the 4-H girl who raised him as a puppy. She was so disappointed he didn't make the guide dog cut, she cried for days. She's now an MP and works with military dogs." Kenzie replied. Lee laughed.

"Amazing how life works out."

"I don't know what I'll do when Flower has to retire. They can only work for about eight years, and he is seven now."

"What happens to him?"

"Oh, I'll keep him, but I'll have to decide about getting a new dog. I'm trying not to think about it. Have to get a bigger house, more yard. I don't know. I worry that Flower would get depressed, being retired and then replaced by another dog." Kenzie sighed as she rubbed Flower's ears. Lee rubbed gently between her shoulders, commiserating with her concern.

"How about that bike ride?" Lee changed the subject.

"Let me go change, and I'd love to." Kenzie hurried into the house. Lee loved riding bikes. They'd gone several times, and he often rode to work. He would be perfectly suited to city bike patrol. She loved watching him ride, muscles working, and sheer enjoyment on his face.

With a pat for Flower, the two left to ride in the warm summer afternoon, enjoying the day, each other, and the sheer pleasure of doing something active.

Chapter 6

Several weeks later, Kenzie and Lee were again eating dinner together. Sometimes, it seemed that all they did was eat or exercise. Still, their time together was limited and eating, and exercising were necessities, except on his Wednesday and Saturday nights doing whatever he so mysteriously snuck off to do.

It was Kenzie's night to pick a movie, and Lee was good-naturedly sitting through an unabashedly gooey chick flick. On his nights, Kenzie suffered through the boredom of documentaries. Lee especially liked the ones about unsolved crimes. She had teased him about busman's holidays, and he had shrugged and agreed. Kenzie generally managed to get bored within the first ten minutes and used the time to snuggle against Lee and enjoy some eyelid fantasies of her own devising.

"What are you doing... Never mind." Kenzie began during a particularly slow scene and then stopped, remembering that every Saturday was reserved.

"What?"

"I wanted to see if you were busy next weekend, but I forgot about your Saturday mystery commitment."

"I actually don't have a...er mystery commitment this weekend. I'm off all weekend, then I go to night shift Monday."

Lee's tone was reserved. The plot on the TV picked up again, and Kenzie fell silent. When things were again at a slow point, she returned to the weekend plans.

"I have a K-day Saturday, so I'm not at the station next weekend."

"A what day?"

"K-day. It stands for Kelly Day. Kelly's the guy who thought it up. Every thirteenth shift, we get a paid 24 hours off."

"Must be nice."

"Yeah, well, what happens is, after 12 shifts, you'll have worked 24 hours too many, and it's either 24 off with pay or overtime. And since no one wants to pay overtime, it makes for a nice firefighter perk."

"We just get told, so sorry, but it's the budget crunch, and we can't hire any more deputies, so you have to work more hours."

"Should have been a firefighter."

"I thought about it. But I really do like law enforcement."

"Arson investigation, then. We can always use more law enforcement."

"It's something to keep in mind. Fire is...."

"Entrancing." Kenzie offered.

"Mesmerizing." Lee's voice trailed off. He watched the TV for a few moments without seeing the screen.

"Anyway, I'd like to go camping next weekend, since my next K-day won't be until it gets too cold and hunting season starts. Would you be interested?" Kenzie asked.

"Car camping or hike in?"

"Either. The car's a little easier."

"That would be fun. I could get off at three Friday. Do you want to leave then?" Lee asked, and Kenzie nodded.

The intervening week passed at a pace approximating continental drift. Kenzie packed and repacked, planned and replanned every facet of the trip. She wanted everything to go perfectly. JohnB teased her unmercifully on the Wednesday before the big camping trip when Kenzie's attention was focused anywhere but the fire station.

"Dr. Livingston, I presume." He interrupted her while she rethought meals with all the concentration of someone planning to take elephants over the Alps. "You aren't going to the North Pole, Kenz. This is just an overnight camping trip."

"No, it's not."

"You spend, what, two, three nights a week together, 'most every week? This is just a camping trip." JohnB pointed out. Kenzie kept her eyes on her notepad. John raised an eyebrow. "Kenz, tell Uncle John all about it. This isn't just a camping trip because...." He trailed off invitingly. Kenzie gave up, knowing that she would have to give him something or he would badger her unmercifully.

"You dope. This is not just a camping trip; it is a planned seduction." Kenzie snapped. JohnB roared with laughter.

"You're the only woman I know who'd go camping to get laid. Most women use satin sheets and lingerie."

"They didn't work," Kenzie muttered, ears turning red. John stared at her in amazement.

"Oh, my poor little Kenzie. I'd have paid money to see that scene."

"It'd cost you more than you make in a decade." Kenzie frowned. John sat in silence for a few minutes.

"Maybe he's gay."

"So maybe I should introduce him to you. Geez, Stinky, maybe he's shy. Or clueless. Or he isn't interested." She added glumly.

"Uninterested guys don't spend as much time with a girl as he does with you. Or send her flowers. No point if you're not looking to get laid."

"Which I've offered, and he's not taking me up on."

"I can always take Lee out for a beer or two and drop a few hints."

"I can manage on my own, thank you very much. Anyway, he's mine."

"Apparently not."

"Go away and let me obsess some more. You are taking all the fun out of it."

"I expect a full report Tuesday." JohnB walked out of the bay and into the kitchen. Kenzie glared after him. Hopefully, he would keep his mouth shut, or she would never live this down. He would probably replace all her station bedding with bright red satin sheets and let her explain that to the chief.

Friday at three-thirty came. Then four and still no Lee. Four-thirty. Kenzie considered working herself into a frenzy. If this was a sample of what some of her more conventionally employed boyfriends had felt about the fire service, Kenzie briefly regretted her sharp responses to their complaints. By five, she had washed every dish in the house and scrubbed the bathrooms to the point she would be willing to eat out of the tub or, even more daringly, the sink. When the doorbell rang, she raced down the stairs three at a time.

"Where have you been?"

"Working."

"I was worried sick."

"Would you just drop it?" His voice was tense. Not the time

for discussion, then. Kenzie reached out and took his hand. Wordlessly, she led him to the couch and sat down beside him. They sat in silence, shoulder to shoulder for a while, Flower resting his head on Lee's knee and gazing soulfully up at him. The dog even had the sense not to thump his tail. Whatever was riding Lee seemed to slowly leak away. He rubbed his hands over his face.

"Still want to go camping?" Lee asked.

"If you feel up to it."

"Yeah. It'd be good to get away. Sometimes I swear law enforcement is about nothing but drugs. Drug houses, gang fights, dead kids. You wouldn't believe the stuff I see." Lee closed his eyes and leaned back, one hand gently stroking Flower's ears.

Kenzie bit her tongue. It was true, firefighters did not see as much of the drug scene that law enforcement did, but they got to see enough, usually cleaning up after law enforcement. After a few minutes, she realized he had fallen asleep. She sat quietly, watching over him. Like all men, being asleep brought out the little boy in his face, and she felt a great welling of emotion. She itched to trace the planes of his face but did not want to disturb him. John would have a good laugh over this, she sighed softly. When she eventually decided to cover Lee with a blanket, her movements startled him awake.

"Oh, geez. I didn't mean to do that." He mumbled.

"Feel better?"

"Yeah. I'll go shower, then we can go if it's not too late."

"No, it stays light until at least nine." Not to mention that there were a lot of plans that would be severely upset. Lee got up and hurried back to his townhouse. Kenzie gathered up the last few items, including Flower, and waited for Lee by his truck.

In very little time, he came out, and they drove away.

"Thanks," Lee said after about thirty minutes of silent driving.

"For what?"

"For understanding. It's nice to be with someone who's been there. My last...er... Tina could never stand to hear about the bad stuff unless it was really juicy, and then it was almost creepy, what she was interested in." Lee's face colored at the slip of his tongue. For a moment or two, he stared at the road, then glanced at her. His smile was warm and held the hint of something else. Maybe he was just shy, Kenzie thought with satisfaction.

"I'm sure you'll return the favor one of these days."

"Probably."

"Turn here. There's a primitive campground at the end of the road. It usually doesn't get too much use." There were two other tents set up at the campground, each carefully distant from the other. Kenzie and Lee found a site further along the road that offered some privacy from the other campers. Working together, they soon had the tent up and sleeping bags stowed away. Coolers of food would be kept in Lee's truck instead of bear-proof containers.

Flower patrolled the boundaries of the campsite, making sure to mark every bush and tree. That chore finished, he returned to lie under the picnic table and growl at the squirrels and gray jays that were investigating the possible new source of food.

With Flower leading the way, they went for a short hike in the quiet forest. The days were long, and full dark wouldn't be for at least an hour. The late evening was filled with birds searching for a last-minute snack. As dusk fell, the birds quieted as the evening's predators awoke. Up here, there were sometimes encounters with raccoons and other evening prowlers. Kenzie had never seen anything larger than a fox and wasn't too sure she wanted to. Just to make sure Flower did not scare up any large residents, she kept him in close. Still, Flower's nose was enthusiastically searching every rock and hole, sometimes stopping to dig after a mouse.

On the return, Kenzie discovered the charcoal had, at some point, been left out and gotten wet and now did not want to start. Mis-step number two. Kenzie worked over the coals in growing despair. Lee watched in amusement for a few moments.

"Not much of a firebug, are you?"

"I put them out, not start them." Kenzie glared at the obstinate coals. Between Lee's stress outburst and the lousy charcoal, this was not going as planned. Lee went to his truck and rummaged around for a few minutes. He returned with an old oil-stained sheet and a can of starter fluid. He ripped a few strips off, soaked them with starter fluid, built a pile of coals over them, and standing well back, tossed a match onto the pile. The starter fluid caught with a whoop and flash of fire that Kenzie felt from her vantage point five feet away.

"Kind of a.... er...an adventurous way to start a fire."

"A stupid way. But it gets the job done if you need a fire in a hurry."

"And aren't too worried about your hair melting." Kenzie pointed out. Lee grinned at her. She felt her awareness of him ratchet into a whole new gear.

Together, they pulled the items for dinner out of the coolers and set them on the picnic table. From the other campsites, the smell of wood smoke drifted towards them.

"I can start a wood fire in the fire ring if you'd like one." Lee offered.

"I'm okay this way. We can have the smell of a fire without the bother of smoke or putting it out."

"I love watching a fire burn."

"I tell you, you're a firefighter at heart."

"Nope. Law enforcement all the way."

Kenzie poked at the fire, watching the coals grey. Deep in the heart of the coals, red eyes winked and snapped. "My brother says one of the most beautiful things he's seen is a forest fire, late at night when the fire lays down, and they get ready to jump on it. He says it looks like piles of rubies in the dark."

"Have you ever fought forest fires?"

"Spent a couple summers on a Forest Service mop-up crew. They called out every fire team in the West, except ours. It was cheaper to call out the prison crews than pay a bunch of college kids, so we sat on our butts and had the sharpest Pulaskis around."

"That stinks."

"No doubt. I was counting on the hazard pay for college. Instead, I spent the year waiting tables for less than minimum wage. I'd rather fight fires. What'd you do to pay for college?"

"Oh... well.... campus cop. Singing telegram delivery. Stuff like that."

"Are you serious?"

"About singing? Yes. I'll deliver you a telegram one of these days." He waggled his eyebrows at her. Kenzie snickered.

"That will be a day to remember."

Their conversation over dinner covered a remarkable number of subjects. Lee was interested in so many different things that she never tired of talking with him. As darkness fell, they wrapped up in blankets to watch the stars wink on overhead. Kenzie snuggled close to Lee, who wrapped his arms around her.

She could hear the steady, slow thump of his heart under her ear. Her hormones were practically raging out of control, and her heart was pounding with adrenaline. Maybe JohnB was right about Lee. She had almost wrapped herself in gift-wrap and left herself on his doorstep, and now, here they were, chastely watching someone else's fire burn down. Now, that was a dispiriting metaphor. She felt like beating her head against a large rock, or maybe Lee's head against a rock. If he had not caught on by now....

"Kenzie?" Lee said quietly. Her thoughts came to a screeching halt, and Kenzie tipped her head back to look up at his dark eyes. "I'd sure like to kiss you." Her stomach dropped into her toes, just like it did on carnival rides.

"I think that would be a great idea." She managed to say. Lee tipped his head down to meet hers, and Kenzie gave herself up to revel in the moment. His fingers lightly traced down her throat, pausing to feel her pulse. Then they drifted lower, to find her hand and wrap around it. He guided it to his own heart, where Kenzie could feel the pulse racing, keeping time with her own. The kiss continued, long, slow, and deep. He had apparently had some excellent experience. Kenzie gave herself up to the sheer enjoyment of the event.

"Do you want to go inside? In the tent, I mean?" Kenzie murmured after a very long interval and a brief catching of breath.

"That would be a good idea. Otherwise, I think we'll be scandalizing the squirrels. But, um, not Flower. That's just... not really my schtick." Lee murmured into her hair. Kenzie laughed and got up, surprised her legs would even work. This night held some great promise after all. Flower followed her to the truck and got in with a resigned sigh. Lee met her at the tent with another knee-weakening kiss and then unzipped the fly, holding it open for them to slip in. Kenzie heard the fly zip close, and then her world narrowed to one person and no one and nothing else.

It had, JohnB agreed the next duty day, been all worth the effort. Kenzie practically glowed, he told her with batting eyes and a sugary sweet voice. Kenzie just laughed and kept the details to herself.

One problem, Kenzie thought, about being the only female in a crew of males is that, once the testosterone died down, the camaraderie set in. She was every firefighter's sister or daughter, although by now, most of those old-timers had retired. After ten years of service, she could even be a mother to a few of the youngsters. And as the only sister in a house full of ten big brothers, a male visitor had them circling like semi-friendly dogs.

Lee was taking it all with good humor, sitting in the bay on an unexpected Sunday visit. Kenzie had given him a nickel tour, introduced him to everyone, and had escaped with him to the quiet of the bay, only to be followed by JohnB and Kurt. They were clearly intent on making sure Lee's intentions were honorable and most definitely not considering whether Kenzie cared if they embarrassed her socks off. She made faces at them whenever Lee wasn't looking, but they did not take the hint. Station bedrooms were off-limits to visitors, not to mention that the teasing would have been untenable if she had taken him to her room. The lounge was crowded with on duty and nosy firefighters taking an afternoon break. Kenzie sighed.

The radio mounted high on the bay wall toned the signal for station three. Immediately all the teasing came to a halt.

"House fire at 1218 Sage Ridge Road. Occupant reports fully involved." The dispatcher announced. Kenzie wrinkled up her nose. Sage Ridge Road.

"Have we been there?" She asked, catching Kurt's eyes, "That sounds really familiar."

"Nope. Out of our territory. That's three's. JohnB, you live over there?" Kurt replied. Realization dawned on both of them, and they turned to see JohnB's face draining of color.

"Oh. My. God." John managed a whisper. "My house." The two minutes seemed to stretch into hours. The radio reported the engine crew on scene. A surprisingly short time later, they reported the fire out and were now performing an overhaul, ensuring that the fire was actually out and not hidden away, waiting for its chance to blaze up and destroy.

"Maybe it's not too bad. Didn't take them long to get it out." Kenzie offered in a small voice. JohnB gave her a dirty look. "Maybe the chief'd let you off. Just to go check."

"We're already short. There's no way he'd let me go."

"The lieutenant at station three will call you," Kurt said. Just then, someone's cell phone cheerfully playing the theme to Scooby-Doo.

"Great. My new roommate." John answered the phone. Kenzie and Kurt looked at each other in puzzlement. Roommate? Since when?

"Yes, I know about the house. The call comes into station one as well. So, what's the damage?" He listened for a few seconds. "You what?" John's voice would have rattled the hanging hoses in the drying tower. "How? Damn." He repeated that refrain several times, each time getting a little louder. "Not my deck! Damn." John had just finished a redwood deck, complete with hot tub and built-in grill. It was his pride and joy.

Kenzie, Lee, and Kurt exchanged glances. The two firefighters had helped on the deck construction, but they had not had the celebratory bar-be-que and initiation of it yet, and from the sound of it, that was probably on hold. Finally, the conversation ended with him punching the end button and sinking onto a gear locker with a groan, head buried in his hands, cell phone clutched against one temple. Silence reigned. Kurt nudged Kenzie. She was JohnB's best friend. She could take the risk.

"So, what happened?" Kenzie asked hesitantly.

"You know that rookie at Station 4? The really dumb one who used to volunteer with County? His girlfriend chucked him out a week ago, and he didn't have anywhere else to go. I guess all his friends knew he was a stupid... Anyway, I let him move in until he figures out that his girlfriend's dumped him for good. He and some buddies went fishing this morning and came back with a string of fish. 'Really nice ones,' he tells me. So, they decide to have a fish fry while they watch porn movies and drink beer. Three of them are volunteers with County. Three. All morons. Where do we find these idiots? Anyway, the oil catches fire, and Dumbshit, the rookie, grabs the pan off the stove and runs to the sliding door. Along the way, he slops oil all over the rug and the curtains, and when he gets to the back door, he wings the entire burning pan of oil onto the deck, where much to his surprise, the deck catches fire." Kurt and Kenzie very carefully did not look at each other. Lee was doing his best to keep a straight face, but Kenzie could feel laughter vibrating in his chest as she curled up next to him.

"They didn't want to call the fire department. 'It'd look bad.' The little old lady next door, you know the neighborhood busybody, called it in. He says he got it out before Station three rolled up, but the rug and the curtains are totaled, and the deck is pretty well a loss. He says the fire didn't eat into the floor joists. And the hot tub was a great source of water." At that, Kurt snorted, and Kenzie found herself sputtering. Lee gave up and gave into laughter. JohnB looked insulted for a minute and then joined them.

"I still think I should kill him."

"You use the Scooby-Doo ringtone for him, and you are surprised he burns your deck down. Geez, John." Kenzie managed through her laughs. Lee stood up, squeezing Kenzie's shoulder.

"Look, John, I have to be going. I'll swing past your place and take a look. I'll call Kenzie with a report." Lee smiled down at her.

"Thanks, Lee. That'd save me a whole lot of worry." JohnB waited until Lee was at the bay door, then called out. "What, you're not going to kiss Kenzie? I might have to do it for you." Lee turned, and Kenzie wasn't sure how to take the glitter in his eyes. She aimed a kick at JohnB's shin, but before she could connect, Lee had crossed the bay and pulled her out of her chair and given her one for the record books, complete with bending her backward. Kenzie clutched at him in consternation and then in ecstasy. The bay floor was really hard, and she did not care to be dropped on it while in the throes of passion, not without something soft to... Lee set her back in the chair with a grin and a wink.

"Sorry, fellas. This one's all mine." Then he was gone. Kenzie collapsed back in her chair, feeling faint.

"You know, John, sometimes you are a real jerk." Kenzie managed.

"Yeah, but... I'd like to be kissed like that." He leered at her.

"He's mine. All mine." She cackled her best ghoul cackle.

"And you lost your chance to kiss me about twelve years ago."

"Darn." JohnB's lack of sincerity made Kenzie laugh.

"So, what's my ring on your phone?" Kurt asked.

"Weird Al's Just Eat It," John replied.

"And mine?" Kenzie asked.

"Ride of the Valkyries. Scares the shit out of me every time you call."

"Gee, thanks. Excuse me while I go download a new ring tone for you." Kenzie got up and left the bay. She made it to her bedroom and collapsed face down on the bed. Two days from now was a long way off. When Lee called, his voice rippled with laughter.

"Tell JohnB it's pretty much how Scooby-Doo described it. I think the porch is repairable. You might mention that the rookie is packing as fast as he can. I suggested he move out before John gets home tomorrow morning." Kenzie giggled. She could just imagine Lee doing his cold cop routine, mirrored sunglasses and all.

"Hey, do you have a special ringtone for me?" Kenzie asked curiously. There was a long silence.

"Yes." He answered cautiously.

"What is it?"

"Oh, well... you know. Old Blue Eye's I Did It My Way." He sounded very definitely embarrassed.

"Good grief. The Ride of the Valkyries and I Did It My Way? Well, at least, it's not She's A Barbie Girl."

"Never that. I've had enough of Barbie girls. I'd take you, my own personal firefighter, any day."

"Thanks. I think."

"I'll see you when you get back from your investigation. Love ya, Kenz." The phone went dead before she could respond.

With an excess of emotion, or of hormones, which could quite frankly amount to the same thing, she threw herself back on the bed and wriggled in sheer glee. Too bad she was heading out of town on a major fire investigation. But then again, anticipation was always the best sauce.

On her return, Kenzie's schedule continued its usual hectic pace. She was at the fire station every third day, fire investigations every other day, and with Lee when both were off duty, and she was in town, and he was not away on his mystery appointment. If it weren't for the nights he spent at her house, she wondered if they'd ever see each other. She fired off a quick email as she sat in the fire station bay and worked on her laptop, catching up on reports during downtime at the fire station.

"Station One, two-vehicle collision on Highway 31 across from Christ's Meadow Free Church. Station One, two-vehicle collision..." The dispatch repeated the call. Firefighters began to congregate in the bay. As usual, the rescue unit left first. Kenzie made a quick save on the computer. The last time she had not, the power had blipped on and off, and she had lost a day's worth of work. Kenzie shrugged into her bunker gear and put on her helmet before climbing into the jump seat. Despite Hollywood's love affair with exploding cars, fires were not a common occurrence at car accidents. The bunker gear would help protect her from sharp metal and hazardous fluids like blood.

It wasn't full dark yet, although it would be by the time they were back at the station. At least it wasn't raining or snowing, although it was cold. Winter was slowly tightening its grasp on the city. At least there had not been any heavy snowfalls. Maybe the slow onset would allow drivers to remember that their cars did not handle as well on snow as they did other times of the year.

As they arrived on the accident scene, Kenzie and JohnB craned their heads over the jump seat to see the accident. One car was a new model red hybrid, the other an older model black sedan of a much stockier build. That meant potential severe injuries to the driver of the lighter car and perhaps the passenger as well. The cars had collided on the driver's sides, and the more lightweight car had spun around, so it was next to the heavier car. In fact, the hybrid and the sedan passengers were seated in their respective cars next to each other. Kenzie could just imagine the conversation they were having, providing everyone was conscious. The police department had blocked the road and was directing traffic to crossroads on either side of the accident.

The paramedics were already on their way to the cars while bystanders watched, and a few hardy Good Samaritans welcomed the firefighters with tight smiles of relief. Because the hybrid's front end was smashed and mangled practically into the passenger compartment, they would probably need to extricate the red car's driver, and JohnB pulled the hydraulic spreader, known heroically as the Jaws of Life, from the engine and carried it over to the accident. Kenzie carried a backboard and neck collar to the paramedics. She would make several trips to ensure they had all the medical equipment required.

"Okay, this is the situation." Jeff, the paramedic lieutenant, spoke quickly and quietly to the gathered firefighters, "We've got two women in their forties in the red car. The driver has an open fracture of the femur and some bruising on the collarbone. She is complaining of hand pain, as well. The dashboard has impinged on her, and the doors are jammed. The passenger appears to be uninjured. There are two men in the black car. They are probably drunk, stinks like a brewery in the car. They are pretty bruised up, no seat belts, some bleeding. Be alert for head injuries or internal bleed outs while we get the women out. Everyone is alert and oriented at this time. Let's keep it that way. Stinky, get the car off the driver." Because the woman driver was the most seriously injured, she would receive care first. Femur fractures were life-threatening injuries.

"Kenz, you keep an eye on the men. Get C-collars on those guys." Jeff followed up with his orders. Kenzie nodded and went over to the black car and bent down to look in. Two twenty-something men looked at her. She agreed with the drunk assessment, although head injuries or diabetes could mimic drunkenness. She could see all the way across both cars, all four victims at once. Usually, they were spread out, and the need to be everywhere at once kept the rescue crews trotting back and forth. She backed away, selecting two large C-collars from the pile, and went back to the black car.

"Why isn't anyone helping us? I'm hurting." The driver whined.

"The paramedics have triaged you, and we need to get the others out first. I'm going to put some cervical collars on you, just for precaution. When Station Two arrives, we'll get you out." Kenzie said calmly. "I'll be keeping an eye on you. What's your name?"

"I am so sorry you had to leave your dinners." The woman driver was saying to Chris, the other paramedic.

"Not a problem. It's our job. We need to do a little work on your car before we can get you out." Chris said and stepped back. Kenzie watched appreciatively as JohnB stepped up to the door and rammed the tip of the hydraulic spreader between the door and the post the door closed onto. He started the spreader and pressed the controls. The jaws began to open, and the door latch broke with a loud bang and what was left of the window tinkled soundlessly to the grass.

Chris yanked on the door, but it refused to open. JohnB repeated the operation on the other side of the door and ripped the door off the hinges. Chris caught it before it could fall and pulled it out of the way, tossing it behind the group of firefighters. Another firefighter pulled it out of the way and to the roadside so that no one would trip over it.

From Kenzie's vantage point, she could see the dashboard had crushed down on the driver's lap. The airbag lay limply on her lap like a white garbage bag. Chris and Kurt climbed into the backseat and held onto the steering wheel. JohnB pulled the airbag away, and Kenzie felt a little faint. Car accidents could be remarkably nasty because people came apart in icky ways. Arson was generally much neater, in Kenzie's opinion, except for the occasional body. In this case, a jagged bone stuck up through the skin of the leg. Living bone was yellowish with red streaks, and it was always disconcerting to see a bone where there was supposed to be skin. Jeff ran quick vitals check as JohnB changed out the spreader head for a steering wheel cutter.

JohnB clamped the pincers of the steering wheel cutter around the steering wheel. The cutter whined, and he increased the throttle. The hydraulic power plant screamed, and then the crunch of metal and plastic giving way filled both cars. The steering wheel broke free, and the two firefighters caught it before it could fall on the driver's leg. The driver stifled a scream. Kenzie was glad to see the passenger of the black car was looking ill. Maybe he would think before participating in this stupid drunken kind of escapade again. John took the steering wheel from Kurt and Chris and threw it away from the car. The two firefighters examined the wreckage for a few moments.

"Gonna have to pull the dash off."

"Think so. Bear, get over here." JohnB called to another firefighter.

"Looks like I'm going to be getting a new car." The driver wiped the sweat from her face and tried to smile.

"Might be a good idea," Chris said calmly. Just talking helped the victim to stay oriented and calm.

"Just think, Sue, you can get a different color. Maybe that pretty green we saw the other day." The passenger offered, her voice trembling. Kenzie shook her head minutely. Whoever had come up the old saw about women being the weaker sex and prone to hysteria had not met these two.

"That would be nice." The driver subsided as pain washed over her. The woman's face was white. Shock would be a major issue, and between the femur fracture and shock, the woman was in serious if not critical condition. At least this rescue would go very quickly, not like some that Kenzie had worked on, with upside-down cars smashed to the point of unrecognition. JohnB and the Bear were setting up the hydraulic spreader to pull the dashboard up and out of the passenger compartment.

"How you doing?" She asked her charges.

"I'm hurting, you stupid bitch, you an EMT? I want some morphine." The male passenger snarled at Kenzie. Both men were dressed head to foot in black. Kenzie barely kept herself from rolling her eyes. The tougher they looked, and the more black they wore, the wimpier they were. Show these guys a needle, and they'd faint like the frail specimens they were.

"Alert and oriented, I see. The medics will be with you soon." Kenzie looked up as a second engine pulled on the scene. Station two had arrived. She sometimes privately swore they finished their coffee before responding to calls. However, extra hands were always welcome.

Jeff, the rescue paramedic, climbed into the red car's back seat and slipped a cervical collar around the woman passenger's neck.

"We'll be taking you out as soon as we have your friend out." He said to the woman passenger.

"Will she be okay? My friend?" The woman asked in a very soft voice.

"We have an excellent trauma center here. She'll be going there." Jeff answered carefully. Fire departments had been sued and lost when a firefighter had soothed someone by saying everything would be alright, and then it had not. It made quieting a hysterical patient or family member much harder because even in the throes of panic, the person recognized an evasion as just that. It sometimes made the person that much harder to handle.

"What about us? This is discrimination." The male driver reached towards Jeff.

"Need help?" Paul, a firefighter from Station 2, came up to Kenzie.

"Keep talking to these two. I'll take their vitals. Maybe they'll shut up."

Chris was sliding a backboard between the woman driver and the car seat. She moaned a tiny bit and immediately apologized. When her spine had been stabilized, he and JohnB lifted her clear of the car while another firefighter kept her leg as still as possible.

"Oh, God...." She whimpered. They laid her flat on the ground and began to apply a traction splint to her leg. This would pull the knee away from the hip and pull the thigh's bone back into position and back under the skin.

"Now, this might hurt a little," Jeff said soothingly. The woman whitened even more as the splint did its work. She wiped away tears, leaving a smear of blood across her face.

"Actually, that hurt a lot." She managed. "But it feels better. Sort of."

"We'll get some morphine going once you're in the ambulance. That'll help a lot." Chris said.

"Sue? I'll see you at the hospital. Everything is going to be fine. I'll call your husband." Her friend called from inside the car as the driver was lifted up onto a stretcher.

"Thank you. Please thank your other firemen for me." Kenzie heard the woman tell Chris.

"Is this your purse, ma'am?" Chris pulled a bag from the seat. The woman's eyes glistened with tears, and she verged on losing her control for the first time in what was becoming a very long night. They trundled her away. Paramedics from the hospital ambulance service took over her care and loaded her into the waiting ambulance. In there, they would start an IV and administer morphine before speeding her away.

"Okay, it's your turn," Jeff told the woman passenger.

"What about us? I'm hurt, and I need help. I'm going to call my lawyer in the morning and report brutality." The drunken driver whined. Jeff looked at Kenzie, who rolled her eyes, carefully out of sight of the two passengers.

"We'll be with you as soon as we can," Jeff answered vaguely. "Kenzie...."

"Can you tell me which day it is?" Kenzie tried to distract the two men.

"I'm hurt." The driver whined. "Hurry up." He began to swear, cussing out everyone from his mother to the maker of his car. The use of curse words was a little monotonous, Kenzie thought.

Suddenly, the woman passenger in the red car turned to the driver of the other, sitting a crushed door width from her.

"Will you shut the fuck up!" She snapped and reached across, slapping the young man across his face. Kenzie slid out quickly from her place behind the men, trying desperately not to laugh. Paul turned away, coughing loudly. The story spread quickly to the other firefighters and police officers too far away to have heard or seen the interaction. Kenzie heard a few snorts of laughter quickly suppressed.

"You see that. She assaulted me." The driver whined again, but with even less response from the firefighters.

JohnB hefted the hydraulic spreader with a grin and cut the red car's roof just in front of the doorposts. He and Jeff pulled the roof up and folded it over.

"Out you come." Jeff and Bear lifted the passenger up through the opening and passed her to waiting firefighters who placed her on a stretcher. In a few minutes, she too was speeding away in an ambulance. Now, just the two drunks left.

Dark had fallen while they were working. Someone on the engine flipped the floodlights on, lighting the scene with harsh light. They tended to wash out colors and make everything seem oddly flat. Kenzie always felt like she was working in a dreamscape, with the floods altering reality. Sometimes the oddness made the job easier, especially on fatalities.

Finally, all four victims had been stabilized and removed from the scene. Wreckers hauled away the cars and their assorted pieces while the fire department loaded all their gear and was now free to go. Kenzie climbed in beside JohnB, and they sat in exhausted silence for a few seconds.

"That was one tough lady," JohnB said tiredly.

"Both of them," Kenzie replied. JohnB turned to her with his best church lady face firmly in place.

"Will you shut the fuck up!" He said sharply. In the privacy of the engine, they were free to laugh as much as they needed to.

The snake whispered thoughts into his head. Burning cars is not what Fire wanted. Fire wanted more and larger. She, in her serpent form, was the high priestess of Fire, and he, the acolyte, needed to listen. Each fire he set came with a very special reward, and so setting fires caused him a great deal of pleasure in more than one way. It was so simple. Follow the commands that Fire gave to her, and he would hear Fire more clearly. Together, they would rise like phoenixes from the ashes he would leave behind him.

He wasn't sure that Fire talked to her initially, but he was petrified of the snake, so he did as she commanded, and it was so simple. She filled all his desires, and Fire worshiped her. Setting fires held even more pleasure for him now.

Chapter 7

Winter had arrived with a vengeance. Fighting fire in the cold was not much fun. The water turned instantly to ice except where the fire kept it hot. There were other considerations. Snow and ice storms. Stranded motorists. And all the winter sports that kept people calling 911. But one of the benefits that this winter brought with it was Lee. Someone warm to snuggle with, ski with, and enjoy walks in the snow. He was out this evening, working on some derelict old dirt bike his friend Steve had purchased. At least it kept them out of trouble.

Kenzie came half-awake as her front door squeaked open. Flower's cheerful greeting, heavy tail banging against furniture, reassured her. Heavy footsteps coming up the stairs, and then the bathroom light came on. It was Lee coming home from an evening out. He spent the nights at her house as often as he did his own, the only exception being the mysterious nights. The shower came on. She had almost dozed off when he came out and slid in beside her. Kenzie scooted over to make room.

"Hi, sweetheart."

"Hey. Didn't mean to wake you." Lee sighed in contentment. Kenzie snuggled up beside him, a warm, clean male with a slight overtone of beer, soap, and toothpaste. A very masculine smell. She let one hand drift over his taut stomach, hugging him close. As he drifted off, Lee turned onto his side. Kenzie draped one arm over him and fell asleep.

She woke before he did and lay quietly, thinking and watching him sleep. He was different from her previous boyfriends. Always well-groomed, in better shape than most of the police department, and tanned. She would have expected Doc's kid to be a little more... rugged, a little less concerned with his looks. Oh, well. At least, she could enjoy the benefits of his idiosyncrasies. She watched him for a few moments, almost overwhelmed with love for this man. She thanked whatever she had done right to have earned this turn of the karmic wheel. Eventually, the call of the coffee pot became too strong to deny, and she slipped out of bed and let him sleep.

Downstairs, Kenzie stood looking out over the snowy landscape, sipping coffee and trying to steel herself into going out into the cold and wind. As usual, it was a training day, but at least it was inside. She'd had an arson dog for so long that she could not imagine life without the rigors of keeping his training current. Every once in a while, Kenzie thought she would like to try it. She grimaced, feeling disloyal to her partner. She looked around for him. Flower sat at the front door, staring down at something. Kenzie went over to him and looked down at Lee's shoes, positioned between Flower's front paws.

"Good dog, Flower." She responded automatically to his alerting and gave him a few pets in apology for her disloyal thoughts. "Outside with you." She ushered the dog out. Footsteps on the stairs preceded Lee's appearance in the living room.

"Morning." Kenzie came into the living room and gave him a quick kiss. He managed to look perfect even with hair tousled and wearing sweats. "Spill gas on your shoes?"

"Why?"

"Flower's hit on your shoes. Want some coffee?"

"Sure." He followed her back to the kitchen and sat as she poured a cup for him and sat down. One sleeve looked very bulky under his sweatshirt, and he kept that hand under the table.

"You realize it's been six months since we met?" Kenzie asked.

"Has it really?" Lee looked vaguely guilty, having forgotten this relationship milestone.

"June to December." They had gone to Thanksgiving dinner with the James's. The older couple was clearly delighted with the outcome of their carefully orchestrated introduction. Kenzie had managed to fend off the offer of a "special" candle. Probably a church scene, the bride and all, and not at all what she was ready for.

"That long, hmm? Seems like only yesterday."

"Flattery?" Kenzie grinned at Lee.

"Better than saying it seemed more like an eternity." Lee laughed.

"True. What's up with your hand?" Kenzie nodded toward his arm.

"Nothing." At his gruff tone, Kenzie looked at Lee with a raised eyebrow. He got up and walked to the window, looking out across the snowy yard.

"I was working on Steve's dirt bike after work, and I hit my hand on the exhaust pipe."

"So, what's the big deal?"

"I just don't like to be fussed over."

"I've noticed. Let me look." Kenzie sighed when he refused.

"I need the patient contact hours."

"Fine." He eased the sleeve up. Kenzie winced at the blistered skin running up his fingers and across the back of his hand, and under the bandage.

"I think you'd better go see the doc."

"I'll be okay. It's not the first time." He slid the sleeve back down over the bandage.

"Second-degree burns are nothing to mess with."

"Enough, all right. It was a stupid mistake, and I don't feel like explaining it." Kenzie was taken aback by Lee's hard, unfriendly tone of voice.

"One too many, hmmm?" Kenzie snapped. There was a long pause. Lee glared at her. "I have to go to work with Flower. I'm heading to the airport. Want to come?"

"I'll pass. It was a late night." Lee yawned.

"See you." Kenzie gathered up her training aids and Flower. She hesitated for a few seconds and then dropped a kiss on Lee's head as she left.

When she returned from the two-hour training session, Kenzie found Lee had been busy. Steaks marinated, and potatoes were baking in the oven. The wine was chilling, and a delectable pair of éclairs chilled in the fridge for dessert.

"Oh, wow. I thought you forgot." Kenzie exclaimed.

"I did, but it's not too late to do something special. Look, I'm sorry about being so... difficult about the burn. I just felt kind of stupid, and maybe a little hungover."

"I'll try not to hover. I'm looking forward to dinner," Kenzie said, and Lee gathered her in for a long and mutually enjoyed kiss. As the phone rang, Lee went to answer it, sharing infatuated smiles with each other. They had been dating long enough that a man answering her phone was no longer a shock to her friends or, most significantly, to her parents.

"Just a second. I'll get her for you." Lee covered the mouthpiece. "It's Bob Chu."

"Great." Kenzie rolled her eyes as she took the receiver. "Hey, Bob, what's up?"

"We got what looks like an arson fire. An abandoned building on Fourth and Grandview."

"Sounds like someone got tired of waiting for the city to condemn the buildings down there."

"Maybe. I hope this is a one-off thing. The last thing we need is another serial arsonist."

"Do you need us?"

"No, it was a pretty simple investigation. The fire was set in a closet. The samples will go out tomorrow."

"Ok, then. Thanks for letting me know." She hung up with a sigh.

"Gotta go out?" Lee asked.

"No. But we've got an arson downtown on Fourth. Our version of urban blight and someone's finally burned one down."

"One less drug house," Lee said calmly. Kenzie grimaced. Fires took immense amounts of manpower and exposed firefighters to deadly conditions. When it was a legitimate fire, the response was justified, but it was a raging waste of resources and possibly firefighter lives for a deliberately set fire.

He was done with car fires. His heart and soul exalted. Houses were his to burn, and the response was incredible. But no longer. The snake coiled around him, frightening him, promising him all he had ever wanted. Only one fire engine showed up when a car burned, but exciting things really happened when a house went up. He had called out two engines and an ambulance through the power of fire, the power that he alone controlled. He had chosen the derelict house because he really did not want to hurt anyone. Just as the snake had promised, the Fire was pleased with him. More than that, he now had all of Kenzie's attention. Just like the snake has promised.

Kenzie sat in a room full of law enforcement and arson specialists, listening to a briefing on the new arson fires. The car fires had stopped, a string of building fires had started, and it wasn't much of a stretch to guess that the car arsonist had upped the ante.

"Our arsonist is using mineral oil and strips of sheet soaked in gun oil." Bob Chu read from the lab report returned on the weekend arson fire. Kenzie scratched her nose while a puzzled buzz filled the room. Mineral oil? Who the heck used mineral oil to start a fire? Well, besides this moron. The gun oil she could see that stuff was as flammable as all get out. For that matter, so was mineral oil. It just wasn't a very common accelerant, and there seemed something very odd about using baby oil to start fires. Usually, it was something a little more obvious, gasoline, kerosene, lighter fluid.

"He appears to prefer empty houses and uses closets or other small, enclosed spaces, so be on the lookout for these indicators when you get called on scene." He discussed other fire-related concerns that law enforcement might need to be aware of, but Kenzie sat thinking of the serial arsonist.

At least now, they'd be getting the resources of the Alcohol, Tobacco and Firearms department. The ATF was called in on all serial fires, and it brought the might and money of the federal government with it. She shrugged on her jacket as Bob finished speaking and left, heading for a fire investigation located in another town.

Chapter 8

Kenzie sat in yet another briefing on the serial arsonist. The ATF people had joined them for several meetings and were now hard at work with federal government arrogance, ferreting out clues the small-town crews might have missed. Bob Chu had been very grumpy over the government handling of the case, but interdepartmental peeing contests were not Kenzie's responsibility or even concern.

"Good news, folks, we've had a sighting of our arsonist. Some kid said he saw a tall, slender man on a mountain bike ride away from the last fire. He had a small dark duffel bag and was dressed from head to foot in black, with some sort of black hat, like a stocking cap, pushed up on his head. The kid didn't see much else. He was late coming home, and he didn't want his grandmother, to quote, "whup his ass.'" Snorts of suppressed laughter met his words. "It's not much, but it's a start, so keep your eyes peeled. God knows how many tall, thin guys riding mountain bikes there are in a university town."

She had driven home, taking note of just how many mountain bikers there were. On that short drive, at least a dozen, including Lee, heading home from the gym by the look of things.

A week or so later, Kenzie sat in her favorite thinking position, feet on the desk and bouncing a tennis ball off the wall. It had taken a lot of practice to bounce the ball and catch it without falling out of a tipped back chair, but dorm life had occasionally been remarkably dull, and odd contests had taken place. This habit was the result of one of them. The phone's ringing broke her concentration, and the ball bounced past her and came to rest under a bookshelf.

"Kenzie, you'll never guess what we found." Bob Chu's voice rang with excitement. She could see him in her mind's eye, striding around his office and gesturing vigorously.

"What?"

"The timing device for our arsonist. It's a gel candle, spiked with gun oil."

"A gel candle. I guess that accounts for the mineral spirits. What will they think of next? Where'd you find it?"

"A patrol officer chased some kids out of a Habitat House on Fifth. He was looking for stolen merchandise and opened a closet, and there it was. A candle scooped out of its container and placed on a rag soaked with gun oil. It had been lit, but the wick didn't stay lit. It's downright ingenious. The wax melts into the rag and burns really hot and slow. The gun oil makes it burn even hotter and kaboom, one hot fire!"

"You are one lucky dog," Kenzie replied with raised eyebrows. She had experimented with gel candles, playing with them in a universal fascination with candles and fire. She had learned two interesting lessons. The first was that spilled wax spread on fire would burn slowly and increase the fire's heat output, and second, that melted gel wax was extremely hot, hotter than normal wax candles and would give second-degree burns where beeswax candles would leave only a moderate burn.

"We are going to nail this bastard!" Bob exulted.

"Not to rain on your parade, but do you know how many people make gel candles?" Kenzie pointed out.

"Yeah." His voice was suddenly deflated, and Kenzie felt a little guilty taking away his excitement. "My wife does. Fake parfaits and liquor drinks all over the house. Fish in candles in the bathroom. Drives me nuts." He sighed.

"It's a great timing device." Kenzie offered in an offhanded way to make him feel better.

"When it works. I gotta go. ATF is breathing down my neck for the report." He hung up.

"Bye," Kenzie said to the dead phone line. She set the phone down and looked at the firehouse scene embedded in the gel candle that Mrs. James had made. The arsonist would not even have to make his own candles. They were readily available at every craft fair and boutique in the city.

Spring arrived slowly, but surely. Tulips bloomed through the spring snows. The arsonist set fires all over town, seeming to prefer the downtown area, Kenzie's district. The ATF was making no more headway than the Police Department and the Fire Marshal's office. On the bright side, Lee was a constant. Kenzie shivered with pleasure and pulled her attention back to the captain. It was finally a warm and dry day, perfect for a little hydrant inspection and painting.

"All right, here's the schedule. Engine One; you'll start on fire hydrant inspection in the Fountain Heights neighborhood. Rescue One, you start inspections at the Fountain Height Mall and that little strip mall north of there. See you back at four." Cap made the assignments.

Kenzie, Kurt, and JohnB went to put their bunker gear in

the fire engine. For this assignment, they could wear station clothes, although it did involve water and paint. Soot marks were one thing on their bunker suits, a mark of service. Paint stains were quite something else, and no one wanted fireplug green on their bunker gear.

Their assignment was to check hydrants and make sure everything was in working order. It also served to remind the crews where every hydrant in their district was located. While they were out, enjoying the spring day, the rescue truck would conduct inspections on local businesses. On a nice day, Kenzie would take hydrant painting over inspection.

At the first hydrant, Kurt unscrewed one of the hose outlets on the side and loosened the stem nut on the top of the fire hydrant with a hydrant wrench. Water flooded out in a great stream. Sometimes rocks or sediments clogged the mains, changed the hydrant's dynamics, and could damage the engine's pump. When he cut the water off, he put one hand over the hose outlet to check for leakage. With the sediment flushing completed, Kenzie took a pitot tube, an obtusely angled instrument with a blade on one end and placed it in the water stream. A gauge in the middle-recorded water pressure. She held it over the hose outlet. Kurt turned the spray on again.

"I read 1,200 gpm." She told the lieutenant who duly recorded the information. Kurt turned off the hydrant and checked the other outlets. Each fire hydrant was color-coded for easy reference of water flow. Fire stations were free to use their own color-coding, but most adhered to the blue, green, orange, red scheme. Blue was the most pressure, over 1,500 gallons per minute. Green was next, followed by orange, and red was the worst, a bare trickle of water.

"Everything looks fine on this one," Kurt told the lieutenant.

He had checked the hydrant for signs of wear and tear, rust, or other problems. Had something been found, the fire station would notify the water department who would repair the damage.

The firefighters also looked for problems with landowners who might try to disguise the hydrant on the corner of their yard with plants or rocks or other decorations. Kenzie failed to see why property owners had a problem with hydrants. Having one in one's yard tended to drastically lower house insurance.

JohnB stepped up and touched up the green paint on the top of the hydrant and the outlet covers, quickly and not terribly carefully. No one gave out awards for most carefully painted hydrants.

Hydrant painting was fun, at least in warm weather. Kids too young to be in school plastered themselves to windows or shyly edged nearer the firefighters, drawn by the allure of the big red engine and water. Law enforcement might get an ego boost by knowing people were slightly afraid of them. Firefighters got a boost from knowing almost everyone was glad to see them. Even the most ardent cop hater generally viewed firefighters as if not heroes, then at least marginally good guys.

They were halfway through hydrant painting when the radio on the engine toned.

"Rescue One, medical call at Washington High School. Student with seizures. Engine One, medical call, Washington High School. Time is 1230." Dispatch called each crew separately since they were not at the station. Kenzie pushed the lid onto the paint can and held out a plastic bag for JohnB to slide the brush in to keep it from drying out. They stowed away the painting materials and climbed into the engine.

"Dispatch, Rescue One responding. Medical at Washington

High School. Time is 1230." The rescue truck crew responded from their inspection across town. The engine crew waited until Rescue cleared the channel. From far away, they could hear the siren starting to wail.

"Dispatch, Engine One responding. Time is 1231." Lieutenant keyed the microphone. Within seconds, they were on their way.

"Final exams?" Kurt asked the lieutenant, whose kids attended Washington High.

"All week."

"Swell." Finals week meant medical calls as overwrought or attention-seeking students collapsed at school.

The rescue truck arrived just before the engine did. A secretary met them at the main doors and escorted the firefighters in. Kenzie and Kurt carried the medical bag and a portable oxygen tank. Students peered out of classrooms, and an excited murmur washed through the halls. Teachers called their students back to order, but there was palpable tension in the air. Kenzie did not envy them the task of recalling over-stimulated students to the task of final exams.

The crew made their way into a classroom where a young girl was lying on the floor, eyes closed. The school nurse knelt beside her, and the rest of the students stood in a horrified herd at the back of the classroom. Kenzie nodded at the teacher, whom she recognized as a fellow exerciser at the local gym.

"What do you have?" Chris asked the school nurse.

"Her name's Tanya. She's sixteen. She doesn't have a history of seizures, according to her records."

"Tanya. Tanya. Can you hear me?" Chris called to the girl. At his words, she began to seize again. Chris waited until she was finished.

Contrary to popular belief, seizing patients rarely choked on their own tongues. The muscles usually would not allow the tongue to slack far enough back to occlude the airway. Also, provided the tongue was behind the teeth, it would not be bitten. A seizing person needed to be protected from falling or bashing into furniture or walls. This girl was in no danger of either. Her limbs were controlled, and, Kenzie sniffed, there was no smell of urine. Epileptics usually voided themselves at the end of a seizure.

Chris checked her eye contraction response while Short Tom, the swing medic, took vital signs.

"BP 110/70. Pulse 80 and strong." Short Tom said quietly. Chris picked up the girl's arm, holding it over her face. He let go, and the arm slid to one side and landed over her head on the floor.

"Kenzie, get me the smelling salts," Chris asked. Before he had even finished his sentence, the girl opened her eyes and looked around in well-simulated confusion.

"Hello, there. Can you tell me your name?"

"Tanya." Her voice was squeaky.

"Where are you, Tanya?"

"English class."

"What day is it?"

"Wednesday."

"Are you taking any medications?"

"No."

"How about anything like marijuana, street drugs?"

"No. I don't do that."

"Have you been sick?"

"No."

"Have you ever had a seizure before?"

"No. It was just so sudden. Everything went dark." She

paused theatrically. "Am I going to the hospital?" She added hopefully.

"The school nurse is going to call your parents and discuss your transport with them. They'll need to meet you at the hospital."

"Oh, no. Please. My dad will kill me if you call him away from work. I'm fine. Really." Tanya's voice lost the squeakiness and returned to its usual timbre. Chris stood up and motioned the teacher and school nurse over.

"I'm guessing this is attention-seeking behavior. We can transport her to the hospital if her parents want her checked out." He said softly so the patient and watching students would not hear.

"I'll go make the call." The school nurse said and left the room. Kenzie and the other firefighters picked up the gear and prepared to leave. The teacher sidled over to Kenzie.

"What's with the lifting the arm and dropping it?" She whispered.

"Someone conscious won't allow their arm to fall full force onto their face. They'll always slide it to one side or stop it before it hits the face."

"No kidding."

"Try it." The teacher stepped back to give the firefighters room to maneuver. "See you at the gym." Kenzie nodded goodbye to the teacher. Leaving the paramedic crew behind to deal with the patient, the engine crew left the building.

"How many more seizures are we going to have?" Kenzie asked rhetorically.

"I did six calls last fall," Kurt answered. Like the flu, seizures seemed to sweep the female population of the high school during exam time. Sometimes, the excitement and attention generated by an actual seizure would inspire others, and there were repeat offenders. Suggesting smelling salts usually would put an end to the fake seizure or faint.

"I'd rather have fake seizures than some doofus with a gun," Lieutenant said. The other nodded. A good number of medical calls turned out not to be emergencies. Some were attempts to get medications without the expense of visiting a doctor; others were attention-seeking; some were panic-driven. The city leaders had discussed charging for false calls to reimburse the city for its efforts, but the fire department had not supported the suggestion. It was better to run a few nuisance calls than to have someone not call for help when it was truly needed, out of fear of being charged for a run.

"Kenzie!" A voice called out from beyond the fire engine. Kenzie peered around the rear of the engine.

"Hey, Gordo." She greeted the tall videographer.

"Anything good?" He asked, hopefully.

"A medical call."

"Are they bringing the kid out?"

"Don't know. You'll have to stick around and find out."

"You're a lot of help." He griped. Kenzie gave him a short wave and climbed into the engine. The press was usually very friendly toward firefighters, but they were still the press.

Chapter 9

After a week of rain, the dirt bike track was a sloppy mess. Kenzie watched the dirt bikes skid around corners and splash down over jumps. At least it just might cushion some of the wipeouts. Sitting in remarkably uncomfortable bleachers and watching noisy two-stroke engines go around and around was not her cup of tea. Still, the companionship, in the form of Lee, was great, and the view was even better. Kenzie eyed Lee appreciatively as he and his friend Steve got ready for Steve's first race.

She slipped her book into Lee's dark blue duffle bag, resting next to her feet, the better to watch. Steve looked like an alien, dressed in pads, helmet, heavy boots, and all the other accouterments of dirt bike racing. Since this was his first race of the day, he was also clean. That would not last much past the starting gate. Much to her relief, Lee did not race; she had seen one too many terrifyingly violent motorcycle wrecks to ever feel comfortable around them, but Lee was Steve's pit crew or whatever they called them in the world of dirt bikes.

Lee was laughing, his head thrown back, and a feeling of complete and total freedom flowed from him. Sometimes he was so constrained by his work and his almost paranoid need for privacy that he forgot to have fun. On this fine spring day, he wore a sleeveless shirt that showed off his impressive muscles in an amazingly breath-taking display. Steve roared off in a spray of mud and exhaust fumes. Lee joined her on the bleachers, leaping up to her level with grace and a quick grin that made her heart skip a beat or two.

He stayed standing to better see his friend. Kenzie watched Lee instead, a more interesting view, to her way of thinking. She could tell when Steve did something terrifying because Lee would cheer, and as he finished first, Lee turned to her for a quick celebratory kiss. Kenzie wrapped her arms around him, going for a much longer and thrilling kiss. Lee responded with all the enthusiasm she could want. Someone started catcalling, and the rest of the crowd took it up. Kenzie felt herself blushing in embarrassment.

"Hey, get a room." Someone called. Lee straightened.

"That's next in my plans." He called back with a grin. "Later, sweetheart. Then we'll do this right and without the Peanut gallery." He whispered to Kenzie. He leaped down with a splash of mud, slipping a little before jogging over to congratulate Steve.

Kenzie sat back with a cat in the cream with a canary on the side grin. The grin faded as she looked down into the pit area. The media was here, in the form of Gordo, followed by Tina. Kenzie snorted. They must have sent her out for a human-interest story—the anchor getting her feet quite literally dirty. Too bad, she looked as though she had stepped out of a Club Monaco webpage. A little mud would do her good. They were also creepily watching her, Tina with a direct but not wrinkle producing expression on her face and Gordo with an expression she could not decipher. Kenzie looked away, focusing on Lee and trying to bring back the feeling of joy that seeing the two had erased.

When Lee came to collect her with a cheerful leer, Tina and Gordo were gone, and Kenzie did not feel it necessary to mention the encounter to Lee.

Three days later, Kenzie set down a stack of newspapers with a sigh. No book. It had to be somewhere, but it certainly was not in the house. Nothing was quite as irksome as getting almost to the climax of a story and then losing the book. Kenzie looked around her house. She had had it a few days ago when she and Lee had been at the motocross race. Stuck it in his bag. She had been pleasantly distracted when they had arrived home and, in a hurry, to get into the house.

Therefore, it had to be in Lee's townhouse or truck, stuck in his duffle bag. He was on duty and would be until late. Kenzie peered out the window, down the street to his townhouse. His truck was parked in his driveway, so he must have biked to work. She walked down and looked through the passenger windows. Nothing. She moved to the topper windows and shaded her eyes to better see inside. The duffle bag was tossed carelessly in the bed. Good. Now she could stop housecleaning and get on with the far more enjoyable task of reading. She moved to the tailgate where Flower was sitting in his alert mode, staring fixedly at the back of the truck.

"Lee spill some gas?" She asked idly as she opened the tailgate and topper door. Flower whined and shifted position. "Show me better," Kenzie said out of habit. Flower put his paws on the tailgate and stared at the box next to the duffle bag. Kenzie frowned and eased one side of the box open, then the other. For a few seconds, she stared down at the contents in puzzlement, then in growing dismay.

A bottle of gun oil had tipped over and leaked into a small wad of torn up rags. That had been the trigger for Flower's interest. Two gel candles had been tossed in the box. One of them had soot around the top; the other was partially empty. Kenzie recognized one of Mrs. James' early works, the colors muddy and swirled together. This one had not been burned, but Kenzie assumed the gel had been scooped out with the plastic spoon peeking out from under the rags. There was a book of matches in the box as well.

Kenzie sat down on the tailgate with complete gracelessness. It was all perfectly innocent, taken separately. Every cop had gun oil and rags. Maybe not kept in a cardboard box with matches. That was a little stupid, but still. The candles were another matter. She could understand burning the dratted things and then returning the containers for a refill that would hopefully be passed on to someone else. She could understand scooping out the gel after the wick had burned completely down and throwing away the leftover gel. But storing them all together in a box. It was the odd combination of all the elements the arsonist used that set off her alarms.

Kenzie closed the box back up and pulled the duffle bag to her. It was black, and she had sworn the one she had seen the other day had been dark blue. Whatever. Blue, black, she had been a little distracted. Kenzie unzipped it and rifled through the contents. Her book was not in it. But there was a pair of black gloves, thin driving gloves, held together by their Velcro. She pulled out more clothing, shaking out black Lycra blend pants that must be absolutely skintight on him. A black long-sleeved t-shirt and under that a black sleeveless t-shirt. Even black socks and shoes. Plus, two containers of hair gel. She turned one over in puzzlement.

Lee occasionally used hair gel to make his hair spiky, but why would he have it in the bag with all the black clothing. He rarely wore black. In fact, she could not remember the last time... except the afternoon she had asked him to go biking. Then he had been dressed head to foot in black. And if she remembered correctly, there had been a fire that night. Her mind replayed an image of him heading out, wearing dark clothes and carrying the bag, so secretive about where he was going. Pretty much what the witness had seen. A tall, slender man dressed from head to foot in black, riding a mountain bike.

Her hands strayed to the box, opening it again, and she looked in it, feeling as though she were rubbernecking at a gruesome accident. Kenzie felt panic start at her toes. She shoved everything back into the bag, zipped it, and threw it behind the cardboard box. She slammed the tailgate up and topper down. It was all she could do not to run back to her house. Flower followed, unable to figure out why he had correctly identified an accelerant and not been rewarded with a squeaky toy or treat.

Kenzie fled up to her office and shut the door. It was all perfectly innocent. He had a reason to have each and everything in his truck. Gun oil and rags for cleaning his service revolver. Gel candles from his mom. Matches. Everyone had matches in their car, house, backpack, although it was rather careless to have them in with an accelerant. Lee was a lot more careful than that. But the gloves and hat. The black clothing. And the scooped-out candle. Her brain spun as if it were on ice.

Kenzie gathered all the investigation notes and newspaper clippings on the arsonist together and found her calendar. Opening her computer calendar program, she started entering dates. Part of her mind was cold and clear. Her job was to find an arsonist, and she would use any and all clues to do so. The other part of her brain, the part most closely connected with her heart, screamed in dismay. She ruthlessly suppressed it.

The fires started randomly at first. Sometimes at night, sometimes during the day, all around the city and even into the county. Towards the middle of summer, the fires settled into a pattern as predictable as her 24 on 48 off schedule. They also started congregating in Station One's territory, Lee's usual patrol area. Kenzie opened her datebook and turned the pages slowly back, entering yet more dates into the computer. The arson pattern emerged after their first date at the restaurant where they had met Tina. The week after, in fact.

Once the pattern had settled down, the fires were generally started on Wednesdays and Saturdays, but only those on which she was on duty. That much she had known and had mapped in an effort to predict the next fire. If they happened on another day, it was invariably also a duty day for her. Never on a Kelly Day when she was off. Once or twice on a sick day. Not on the camping weekend, she noted. And never when Lee was on second or graveyard shifts. Almost like someone had known both their schedules. Circumstantial.

She entered the first house fire date. It had happened night Lee had shown up with the burn on his hand and arm. It had looked like an exhaust pipe burn. It also could look like a back flash, she realized, with the accelerant popping up his fingers and arm. She buried her head in her arms. This was all a bad dream, and she would wake up soon. But no. The clear light of day did not change when she lifted her head. Not a dream. But a nightmare, nonetheless. A giant logic puzzle, and she was stuck in the very middle of it. Kenzie saved her findings, copied them to a flash drive, and shut down the computer. She hung the flash drive on a cord around her neck, tucking it inside her shirt. It felt like a betrayal, but of whom she could not tell. Carefully, she put all the notes away and went out, closing the door behind her with great care.

Her next move could determine her entire future, and Kenzie wanted to think very carefully before acting. Never before had she been in a situation where both her career and personal happiness had been on the line. It was an uncomfortable place to be. Sometimes being a woman was not all it was cracked up to be. Catch-twenty-twos lurked around each corner, and this was one huge dilemma. If she said nothing, did the "stand by your man" thing, public judgment would be that she was a poster child for why women did not belong in the fire service in a man's world. A man would have turned in his girlfriend. But if she turned him in and violated that powerful expectation of loyalty to her man, public judgment would call her less of a woman. No matter what she did, she would be wrong.

Lee was very late coming home from work, and she was happy that he did not come over.

The next day, a Wednesday, Kenzie drove to work and took a personal day off. JohnB reluctantly and suspiciously agreed to cover for her if Lee stopped by or called the station phone. She rode her bike home, sneaking in the back way and discovering that climbing a six-foot fence was not as easy as it had been four years ago when she had last locked herself out.

Kenzie took care to stay away from the windows and avoided any appearance of occupying the house. It was harder than she expected to leave all the lights off and not rush out to get the mail and paper when they arrived. Distracted and irritable, she finally had to give up on writing reports because of the number of errors she was making. By evening, her nerves were wound to a fever pitch, and after she had snapped at Flower for no reason, the dog slunk off to hide until his adored person regained her sanity.

Finally, Kenzie was reduced to sitting with her head in her hands. The data ran through her mind, each replay more damning. Tonight, Lee would be gone to wherever he went on Wednesday. If there was only some way to follow him. But Lee on his bike was formidable, and Kenzie knew she could not keep up on her bike, and as for tailing him in a car, she had her doubts about her success. That would be for someone else more experienced at tailing. Driving big red fire engines did not give one the necessary skills for sneaking quietly after someone.

Kenzie turned on her fire scanner and sat where she could see the street. And then she waited. Lee came home. A little while later, he biked past her window, black duffle bag swinging from one handlebar, and was gone down their street. The regular traffic came and went through dispatch. She was missing an evening of injuries, from the sounds of it. It was getting very close to the time that Lee usually came home from wherever he went.

"Station Two, house fire on 211 West Elm. House fire 211 West Elm. Time is 2100." The dispatcher's calm voice crackled the fire scanner to life.

"Station Two responding to house fire 211 West Elm. Time is 2100." The Station Two lieutenant responded. Kenzie was reasonably familiar with the area, and she was pretty sure the building was derelict. At the rate the arsonist was going, he would have to switch to inhabited homes to keep up his habit. Kenzie shivered at the thought.

An hour or so later, Kenzie saw Lee's bike turn down their

street. He was riding slowly, tiredly. Her hands clenched, digging fingernails into her palms. Tomorrow he would be over after work. She would settle this tomorrow.

Kenzie went upstairs to go to bed in the dark. It was early for her to go to bed, but there would be no telltale lights or shadows. All she needed was Lee coming to investigate an intruder. Of course, he might accidentally shoot her and save her the trouble of turning all this incriminating evidence over to Bob Chu. But he was too good a cop for that. Kenzie threw herself on the bed and screamed into her pillow. Sleep eluded her.

Early the next morning, she rode her bike to the station and picked up her car. JohnB did his best imitation of big brother, crossing his arms with hands under his biceps and glaring down at her. Normally that would have reduced her to helpless giggles, but today she was too tired and heartsick.

The day was as endless as the previous night had been. The investigations went on, as people played out their own little dramas that had nothing to do with hers. The two-hour drive to the house fire she was investigating gave her ample time to fret. This fire was in a threatened foreclosure. Lose a house and ruin a credit rating or go to jail for arson; now there was an attractive set of choices—kind of like hers. Kenzie growled to herself.

At home that evening, Kenzie waited on the front step until Lee drove up. He tooted the horn cheerfully, and she waved back. After Lee had parked, he walked over with a grocery bag in his hand. He held the other out to her, drawing her to her feet for a long and heartfelt kiss.

"Nice night." Lee grinned at her. Kenzie sniffed surreptitiously. Only the smell of a day of work. No smell of smoke or accelerant, but then her nose was not as good as Flower's.

"I have provided dinner." He held up the bag and shook it invitingly. "Can you provide the beverages?"

"Sure. I've got iced tea or pop." Nothing stronger, although if there was a night for alcohol, this was it.

"Tea, please. Bring it with you." Lee waited until Kenzie came back out with the pitcher. "Busy day?"

"Something like that. Had another arson fire last night. Or so we are assuming. On west Elm."

"Abandoned house? At this rate, he'll have single-handedly cleaned up all the derelict properties."

"And then what? Inhabited houses?" Kenzie snapped. She shook herself mentally at Lee's raised eyebrows. "So, what happened today?"

They talked of the day's events while Lee dished out dinner and poured the tea. Kenzie wandered over to the kitchen window, where a selection of gel and soy candles sat. Collecting dust, she noted. Picking one up, she turned it over in her hands.

"I think you have more of these than I do. Do you ever burn them?"

"You kidding? With this many candles, I'd probably set off the smoke detector. I'd have to burn them all day, every day to use them up, and that would be bad for my manly image. Plus, they stink." Lee winked at her. "When I get too many, I ship them to a friend who owns a crafty boutique in the city. She sells them, and I donate the money to the Widows and Orphans Fund. Makes everybody happy."

"There's an idea," Kenzie responded vaguely, but to which idea she did not specify. Lee laid out sandwiches and chips and looked expectantly at her.

"You're in a bad mood today. What's up?" He asked kindly. It was enough to undo her, she thought grimly. Now or never.

Kenzie took a deep breath.

"Where do you go on Wednesdays? And the other days? When you just disappear?" She watched as the happiness in his face congealed and then faded away.

"You wouldn't believe me if I told you."

"Try me." Kenzie offered. She picked up a sandwich and toyed with it.

"No. Look, it's nothing important—just something I do for fun. I'm not hurting anybody. But it's something I don't talk about."

"Why not?"

"Because I don't. I think this conversation has gone as far as I want to take it." His voice was flat. Kenzie considered her options.

"Please. It's important." She put her sandwich down.

"So is my privacy."

Kenzie shoved her seat back and stood up, looking down at him. He looked back blandly, but under that neutral expression, his eyes were hard. He was so very beloved, sitting at his dining table, the ruins of dinner spread across it. So many evenings they had spent together. Lee made no motion to stop her as Kenzie went to the door and opened it.

"Goodbye, Lee." She shut the door quietly and went back to her own house, feeling her world fill up with cracks. All she needed was one more stressor, and it would shatter at her feet.

It was a couple of days until she could get to the fire marshal's office. Life and procrastination gave her an excuse not to take that long walk. As she went down the hall from the fire station to the fire marshal's office, she was still arguing with herself about turning over all the evidence. Her first words were curt and to the point.

"I have a problem." Kenzie walked into Bob Chu's office and closed the door behind them. Flower's nails clicking on the linoleum were loud in the sudden quiet. He looked up at her in surprise but what he saw in her face stopped the tart comment he would typically have made.

"What's wrong?"

"I have a whole lot of odd coincidences that add up to a possible arsonist. The one who's been setting those house fires. I don't know what I should do."

"That should be obvious." Bob Chu looked at her curiously.

"It's not that easy. I have no solid proof, just a bunch of circumstances, matching dates, and that sort of thing. And it's someone... it's a friend."

"Who is it?"

"Lee James." There was a very long silence. Kenzie felt her heart shriveling inside her.

"Isn't that your boyfriend?" Bob's eyebrows rose to his hairline, a neat trick considering how far up it was.

"Yes," Kenzie whispered. Bob Chu tapped his pen on the blotter a few times.

"And he's a police officer?" He asked. Kenzie nodded. He pursed his lips and looked down at his blotter, drawing a small design in an empty corner. He looked back up at her. "I begin to see your problem. Show me your evidence."

"I was looking for something, a book I was reading, and thought I left it in his truck. When I went to get my book, I found a box full of gel candles, gun oil, and old rags. I know his mom makes candles. I have at least a hundred of hers at my house. Lee's got even more at his. I know he uses gun oil regularly, obviously. And Lee is very neat, so I can justify the rags as well. I found a black duffle bag filled with black clothing like the witness described, and he rides a mountain bike and fits the physical description. I charted the fires against his schedule, and they fit perfectly. He goes somewhere almost every Wednesday and Saturday night, and almost every fire started on those nights. Look at this." She handed the flash drive to Bob, who inserted it into his computer and opened it in silence. He studied the calendar carefully.

"It's still all circumstantial."

"The morning after the house fires started, he came home with a burn on the one hand. He said he got it from an exhaust pipe on a motorcycle. Which is possible, I suppose. He does work on motorcycles with his buddy Steve what's- his-last-name with the Highway Patrol." She fell silent again. Arsonists had been caught in hospital emergency rooms where they had gone to be treated for burns.

"Still thin."

"Lee's really interested in what Flower can and can't smell and how he works."

"He's your boyfriend. I'd guess he is interested in you more than the dog." Bob said dryly.

"I've thought of that. Lee doesn't fit any of the profiles, either."

"Ever seen him at any of the fires?"

"No, but then my own mother could be at a fire, and I wouldn't see her. Things are pretty hectic." Kenzie sighed. "Gordon Ellis at Channel 4 sends me footage of fires he works. And sometimes photographs if he's not officially on scene. I've studied the crowd shots over and over, and I couldn't find any regular watchers."

"What does Flower think about him?" Bob asked. Kenzie

unconsciously put her hand down to pet the dog.

"They get along great. But I've seen Flower hit on Lee's shoes or clothes. His truck. And his bike." She added slowly, remembering.

"Which is all easily explainable. Lee dribbled when he was filling the tank or rode through spilled gas." Bob thought for a while; his eyes were drawn back to the computer screen. "So, how are you guys getting along?" He asked innocently.

"Oh, come on, Bob. This is not some sort of macabre revenge plot. I almost didn't come in to talk to you because I do not want it to be him. But I had to. It all fits, almost too well." Kenzie snapped. Bob had the courtesy to look abashed.

"Okay, Kenz. I had to ask. Look, so far, the financial damage has been fairly insignificant because they've all been abandoned houses and that one drug house." Bob looked thoughtful.

"That could very well be a law enforcement motive. Has anyone else had a rash of arsons similar to these?"

"Not to my knowledge."

"Ok. This is flimsy, but it's the only lead we've gotten. You call the fire departments wherever Lee has been employed and see if they've had a string like this."

"Ok. I'll let you know in a few days."

"The ATF will be dropping in to visit about our arsonist in a few days. Before they get here, I'll call the police and talk to the chief. Don't say anything to anyone. And be very careful."

"Oh, believe me, I will. I didn't... It can't be Lee. I can't explain away the coincidences, but it can't be Lee."

"Can't be or don't want it to be? Ask your friend at Channel 4 if he'll take more crowd shots at the next fire. I'll try to get to the next one and take some of my own."

"I'll ask him. He was big into press privilege and not helping law enforcement without a warrant when we were in college."

"Then why's he sending you photos?" Bob asked. Kenzie shrugged.

"I assumed it was, so I'd like him better. Not much in the way of social skills." She let herself out, closing the office door quietly behind her.

Chapter 10

ee was sitting on her front step when she got home. Kenzie watched him for the few seconds it took to turn off her vehicle and gather up her belongings. The part of her that still believed in miracles, and happy endings was glad to see him. As for the rest, she sighed and let Flower out of the truck. The dog rushed over to Lee, wagging his tail madly. Lee petted him a few times before standing up so he would be on the same level as Kenzie.

"Are we still talking?" He asked in that deep quiet voice that gave her shivers. In one hand, he held her door key but had not used it. Respecting her privacy, Kenzie thought with a slightly hysterical mental giggle.

"I suppose. Look, Lee, I'm sorry. I'm exhausted, and I just want to go to bed."

"I'll go with you. Give you a back rub." He leered cheerfully at her. One last time, she thought. What would it hurt, besides her heart?

"You're on." She unlocked the door, and they went in together, Lee's hand resting casually on her back. Kenzie shivered. He felt so perfect.

Kenzie turned over to an empty space in her bed, feeling around for Lee but finding no one. She slit her eyes open. Early dawn, almost time to get up anyway. Lee came in from showering, and she watched him dress. Undershirt, underpants. Socks. Pants. Shoes. Kevlar vest. Shirt. Duty belt. Hair mousse. Kenzie turned a snort of amusement into a snore, but Lee was not deceived. He came over and bounced on the bed.

"Rise and shine, sleeping beauty. Time to go catch bad guys. Or bad girls, as the case may be." He planted a kiss on her.

"You're in a good mood." Kenzie hugged him, sneakily sniffing the smell of his cologne.

"What could possibly go wrong? See you tonight." He left singing the chorus from *Good Life*, his hands and feet beating out the drum line as he went down the stairs. The door slammed behind him, and all was quiet.

"What can go wrong? How about your girlfriend selling you up the river?" Kenzie muttered to the silent room. Life was just ducky.

Kenzie made the calls to fire services in Lee's former duty stations. The fire marshals had a sprinkling of unsolved arsons to be expected in a town of any size, but no strings of MOs matched with hers. Not that that meant anything. Sometimes arsonists took years to come into their own, starting with socially acceptable fires in barbeque grills before accelerating to unacceptable ones. It made her feel marginally better, but there was still a pile of circumstantial evidence and unanswered questions.

"What's going on with you and Lee?" JohnB asked as they cleaned up the fire engine after a call.

"Nothing."

"Tell me another one, Kenz. You're running around like a

bear with a sore head and jumping all over me if I mention Lee or anything that remotely reminds you of him. Which is pretty much everything."

"Nothing's wrong." Kenzie polished the chrome bumper with extra vigor. JohnB put his hand on the rag, stopping her.

"I haven't ever seen you happier than when you are with him, or talking about him, or thinking about him. He's a good man, and he's good for you." JohnB's voice was quiet. Kenzie stared very hard at the winch on the bumper, willing away the tears. She had never given JohnB the satisfaction of reducing her to tears when he tortured her back in the bad old days. She would not cry when he was kind.

"I think I've screwed the pooch on this one, John, and nothing is ever going to be right again." She threw down the rag and went to her room. John sighed and picked up the rag, taking up where Kenzie had left off.

Evening had come early, winging in on an oncoming storm. Kenzie and Flower scurried up to the house as the first few raindrops pelted down. She hated coming home to a dark house, and timers usually turned on the lights. Kenzie unlocked the door and flicked on the light before coming all the way into the room. A sudden movement on the stairs startled her, and she whipped her head up. Adrenaline flooded her system.

Lee was standing at the foot of the stairs. His eyes glittered with rage, and his frame was tight. He was still in uniform, and his Kevlar vest made him look even more massive and threatening. His hands clenched on a cardboard box, and Kenzie could see the box starting to cave under the pressure. Flower came rushing in, barking. He stopped when he saw Lee and looked uncertainly from one to the other. The dog was very aware of the tension waving off his human and equally aware that Lee was no stranger. Kenzie opened her mouth to say something, but her voice refused to even squeak out.

"You...." Lee growled out the word, making it an epithet. He was so angry that words failed to form. The muscles in his jaw clenched. "I go into work today, and what do I find? The goddamned ATF, the police chief, and your buddy, Bob, the fire marshal, all waiting for me. And why? Because I'm suspected of arson. You ...." His voice rose to a roar.

He stopped and glared at her for a few long heartbeats. Kenzie could feel hers pounding in her chest: no great measure of time. The ten rapid beats felt more like an eternity.

"I am suspended, Kenzie, until a formal investigation is completed." He had his voice under control again. "And do you know why? Because my girlfriend," he snarled the word, "accused me of being an arsonist."

Kenzie stayed silent. There was nothing to say, and possibly, if she spoke, it might release a more vicious attack. She backed slowly towards the door, not wanting to be trapped in the house with him. Lee watched her, his upper lip quivering into a snarl.

"Don't worry. I don't set fires, and I don't hit women. Even ones like you." He shoved past her, shoving the screen door open with his box. Kenzie had been so very afraid of this moment and had known it was inevitable from the second she had laid her suspicions on Bob Chu's desk. But that did not make it any easier. Lee came back in and went up the stairs. In a few minutes, he came back down, clothes draped over his arms.

"What in the hell did I do to deserve this? I have served with distinction for twelve years. Never a breath of scandal. And then you come along. You.... What were you thinking? Was it just your day to ruin my life? You couldn't just ask me?"

Kenzie cleared her throat, "I did. During our last conversation at your house. You blew me off." Lee looked at her for a moment, eyebrows creased in confusion.

"A week ago?" His eyebrows lifted. "Oh-ho, the leading questions about gel candles. Not to mention my whereabouts. Is that what this is about? That conversation? And you've been screwing me since?"

"Lee...."

"Are you some sort of jealous of my not spending every waking minute with you? It seems like I spend plenty in your company."

"Oh, give me a break. I asked. You got all secretive. All I had to go on was my evidence."

"Wild-assed speculation. I thought you'd be different from Tina. Was I wrong? At least she was upfront in her underhandedness."

"How did Tina get into this conversation?" Kenzie asked, bewildered. Lee glared at her.

"Maybe if you weren't so secretive, I'd understand a whole lot more than I do right now. Every fire started when I was on duty, and you were at your mystery engagement. During the exact times you were gone."

"Thanks to you, I'm going to be the laughingstock of the department."

"I did my job."

"No, you didn't. You have screwed up royally. And let me enlighten you on a few facts, Kenzie since reasoning is apparently not your strong suit. I am a law enforcement officer. Do you understand what that means? I enforce the laws. I do not break them. Second, I am not and never have been an arsonist. And finally, you can rot in hell." He made each word separate and complete. He shoved past her, reached back to grab the door handle, and slammed the door.

Pictures rattled on the walls. Now that would be a fine counterpoint, the gentle tinker of shattering glass. Kenzie steadied the closest picture and listened to the silence until Flower whined. She glanced down at the dog and soothed the soft silken ears down.

"You're a good boy, Flower." Then she walked through the house. The closet gaped open. Uniforms and civilian clothes that had collected there over their relationship were gone. Lee's books were gone from the bedside table. The medicine cabinet was empty of toothbrush, mousse, cologne, and shaving cream. Every trace of Lee's occasional residence was gone. With a mild oath, she turned and went into the office. Its order and neatness with no sign of anyone but herself was reassuring.

Kenzie contemplated going down to Lee's house and trying to talk to him. She had done her duty, as hard as it had been to suspect him. She doubted there was anything she could say that would make a difference, and anyway, he was a suspect, and her associating with him could very well be a huge mistake. Kenzie closed her office door and went downstairs. There was nothing else to be done.

Three days later, she knew that word had gotten around about the entire fiasco. Driving into the station parking lot, she passed a police car driving out. Her habitual wave was ignored. The dark glasses turned her way glinted in disapproval. Heaven help her if she ever needed law enforcement now. She had better hope to not get a speeding ticket or even a traffic violation, or she would find herself in a world of trouble. JohnB met her at the bay door when she pulled it open.

"The jungle drums say you accused Lee of being the arsonist, Kenz." JohnB cornered her, eyes glinting, and voice gone harsh. "Are you insane?"

"Yes. Leave me alone." Kenzie hunched her shoulders. She shoved past him and went to her room to unpack her bedding. When she walked into the crew room, the assorted firefighters stared at her in varying degrees of disbelief. Two turned away in disgust. The room was as unfriendly as it had been ten long years ago when she had been the girl rookie, unwelcome and unwanted. Kenzie reached down deep inside herself to the old, dimly remembered habits that had gotten her through her rookie year. She straightened her shoulders and looked around at each of her fellow firefighters, then turned to check the chore board.

Her only defense that she was doing what she thought was correct would not hold much worth in her station mates' eyes. A terrible headache started pounding behind her eyes. The duty lieutenant had assigned her all the most disgusting jobs, and Kenzie went off to complete them, trying not to feel as if she were slinking away to hide.

The snake said it was time to stop the fires. Fire had done what they wanted of it. Kenzie was humbled. Now she would be ready to listen to the voice of fire. He knew that. But the snake did not understand. She thought it was about revenge, and she did not understand that the fire held his soul. It was about power. To stop now, his soul would die, and so would fire. One thought repeated itself, fire must not die. He was the god of fire, and he would never stop. Barbeque grills, cars, abandoned houses. It was all a thrill, and he needed the power. Stripped of it, he was nothing.

Three long and chilly days at the fire station interspersed with six of being alone on her investigations followed with painful slowness. Kenzie managed to avoid Lee in their comings and goings. His townhouse had a curiously unoccupied air about it, even though she could see the flicker of blue TV light coming from the living room window as she spent sleepless nights patrolling first inside, then outside her house and the backyard with Flower. When the patrol car reappeared, two weeks later, in his driveway, Kenzie realized Lee's suspension was over. Apparently, wherever he had been, settings fires had not been his activity. The next morning, she was on duty, Kenzie picked up a two-way radio and went down the hall to Bob Chu's office.

"Well?" Kenzie asked. Bob gestured to a chair, and Kenzie sat down. He tented his fingers and looked at her over them, a habit she found disconcerting.

"Lee's alibi checked out for every night, except one, that he could have started the fires. Besides, his alibi is watertight. He's off suspension. And there is no question of doubt in anyone's mind that he is not the arsonist." Bob never pulled his punches. Sometimes it made him uncomfortable to work with. Kenzie looked up at the ceiling, mustering her response.

"What was his alibi?"

"I can't tell you. Lee asked for complete confidentiality and given what a black mark this investigation could have been on his record, I agreed. His superiors are satisfied as well." And you should be satisfied, too, Kenzie heard the unspoken suggestion.

"So, now what?"

"We keep looking." He paused, and when he resumed speaking, his voice was much kinder. "Your reasoning was sound, Kenzie, and all the facts added up to one person. I would have made the same assumptions, and it took a lot of courage for you to step forward, given your relationship with Lee. Don't spend too much time second-guessing yourself." He nodded once, a clear dismissal. Kenzie left the office and went into the women's restroom. Sorrow, frustration, and relief washed over her in equal measures.

"I have second-guessed myself every minute for the last month. And I will second guess myself for the rest of my life." She muttered to her reflection in the mirror. She washed her face in cold water, pasted a smile on, and went out to face the rest of her life.

Several weeks later, Kenzie was sorting out the first aid box, ensuring everything was in order after their last medical call. Things had gotten a little hectic, and some of the contents had been returned willy-nilly. The rest of the engine crew had washed and dried the engine and, continuing the silent treatment, left her to her own devices.

"Hey, Kenzie." Someone spoke softly from behind her. Kenzie turned around to see Gordo watching her. "I've been watching you for the last few minutes. Penny for your thoughts."

Now that was a creepy thought, him watching her.

"Just a lot of white noise." Kenzie replaced the last of the supplies, returned the box to its proper place, and then sat down on the engine's sidestep, just below the pump panel. "What brings you around here?"

"Just wanted to talk," Gordo responded. Kenzie waited, but he said nothing more. The look in his eyes made her feel uncomfortable.

"I need to get back to work." She said finally.

"Yeah, those bandages need rerolling." Gordo's voice was

bitter.

"Then talk."

"Any luck with the arson investigation?" Gordo said quickly. Kenzie reconsidered him for a moment. He had been a friend, more or else for years. But he was also a member of the press corps. His first loyalty had always been to his camera and his career.

"It's progressing as expected."

"In other words, you haven't a clue." His eyes glinted. Kenzie shrugged, allowing him his opinion. "I hear you aren't seeing Lee anymore." Kenzie stood up and turned her back, opening another compartment and rewrapping a blood pressure cuff into a neater package, and shoving it into the bag. "Don't feel bad. Tina and I aren't together anymore, either."

"Sorry to hear that." Kenzie managed.

"Yeah, I couldn't take her jealousy anymore."

"Really."

"You'd think someone that pretty would be nice."

"You'd think." A dozen other equally trite remarks flitted through Kenzie's mind, but she had no interest in continuing this conversation.

"Crazy as a bedbug and mean as an alligator." Gordo continued, oblivious to Kenzie's short answers. Lovely, Kenzie thought, what a reputation to be compared with. She wondered what hers was. Stupid came immediately to mind. So did clueless. Why wouldn't he just go away?

"How about it?" Gordo asked in the voice that one uses when repeating a question for the third or fourth time.

"What?"

"You and me. On a date. I've liked you since Freshman English."

"Not right now, Gordo. I just... don't want to date anyone right now. I'm not ready."

"You have to." Gordo reached out and grabbed her arm. "She said you would."

"Let go." Kenzie's voice went flat. She could hear Flower start barking in her room. Great. That ought to annoy the captain. Just what she needed. He had her by both arms, and she flipped through her options, deciding on a swift kick to the shins.

"It's time you leave." JohnB suddenly loomed up from behind the truck and stood beside Kenzie. He managed to look even bigger than he was, a trick Kenzie decided she needed to learn. Gordo gave the other man a look of absolute hatred.

"So much for not ready to date." Gordo stormed out of the engine bay. The slam of a car door. The scream of an over-torqued engine, the shriek of tires on pavement, and then his car speed away. They waited in silence for a crash of metal on metal that never came.

"How long have you been listening?" Kenzie asked quietly.

"Not long. I actually came out to talk with you about the time Gordo was declaring his undying love." Amusement streaked JohnB's voice.

"It was just a date."

"I certainly wouldn't date him. He has creep stamped all over him."

"Yeah, well, thanks to you, I doubt he'll be back."

"I don't know." JohnB mused, his eyes on some middle distance. "I think he'll be back. You need to be careful."

The snake said it was time to stop the fires. They were getting too close. And if they found him, they might find the snake and that the snake would not allow. But the snake did not understand. The snake thought it was about revenge and did not understand that the fire held his soul.

His hands shook as he emptied another candleholder and laid the rags out so that it would pull the fire away from the candle and into the carpet. A crafty idea occurred to him next, and he sat back, almost distracted by the beauty of his vision. No one suspected him. He had been so very clever. He would stop for a while, find the perfect way to start the next fire, and to hurt the firefighters who would come.

Yes, he had plans, and Kenzie was part of them. And she would regret her every decision, from deciding to be a firefighter to trying to crush him into oblivion. She would pay. He struck the match and lit the wick. He backed out carefully and closed the door on the future inferno. His bike was waiting, and he calmly biked away.

For someone who lived four doors away, Lee avoided Kenzie with an almost perfect record. On the rare occasion that they passed each other, Lee managed the most perfect cuts outside of a Jane Austin novel. Of course, the mirrored sunglasses did not help much. Kenzie cringed every time she saw Lee's truck go by, and she finally started to check out the front window to make sure the coast was clear before leaving the house.

She would move except that finding a rental that allowed dogs was difficult. She would stay put for the time being but having to stay did not mean she liked feeling that she was skulking behind her curtains. The slow weeks rolled past. No arson fires. No Lee. No joy. Kenzie felt as if she were putting one foot in front of the other in a slow and anguished procession.

Chapter 11

"Hoo, baby, Kenzie, you are going to have fun tonight." JohnB kept a firm grip on Kenzie's elbow despite his encouraging words. She hustled a few steps to relieve the pressure point he was grasping with such enthusiasm, shivering a bit in the fall air. It had been six months, and JohnB was attempting to bring her back into the brotherhood of firefighters.

"Unhand me, you brute." Kenzie shook her arm free. "You know, watching some woman take off her clothes doesn't do much for me, bud." Kenzie frowned at him.

"Well, me neither." JohnB assumed a pious expression marred only by the twinkle in his eyes. Or maybe it was just the harsh neon light reflecting off them, Kenzie thought sourly. "This is different." He grinned down at her as they joined the other rowdy firefighters in the parking lot of the Lucky Ladies Adult Entertainment Emporium. Kenzie groaned.

One big drawback of being one of the boys was being treated like one of the boys. She could have stayed home, washed her hair, cleaned her kitchen, but no. The rookie from Station Two was getting married, and they, his brother firefighters, were treating him to a night in the big city. The brother honoraria included one reluctant female firefighter.

Kenzie realized this wasn't a bizarre form of sexual harassment but a genuine desire to include her, even covered in sackcloth and ashes, even in such a ham-handed way. Fortunately for the rookie, this was not his wedding eve; his fiancée had put her foot down about that date, but the weekend before.

Accordingly, they had driven to the big city, eaten too much, and Kenzie was quite sure they would eventually drink too much. With hotel rooms across the street in a sleazy no-tell motel, everyone would be able to stagger to bed from the strip joint and sleep off the excesses. And probably get fleas at the same time. Lovely. Kenzie cast one last longing look over her shoulder to her SUV. She could escape, drive to a better part of town. Find a bookstore. Better still, a coffee shop or, even, stop the heart-pounding ecstasy, both at the same time.

"How is it different? They're still naked women." Kenzie inquired.

"Because you're with us. This is male bonding time. Be one of the guys, Kenzie, and fix a few of the fences you trashed. You aren't exactly Miss Popularity these days." John lowered his voice and pulled her to a stop, serious for a moment. Kenzie rolled her eyes.

"I don't think watching a strip show's going to do much in that department."

"You never know. Come on."

The bouncer eyed the group of men with one lone woman curiously as he checked their IDs and took their cover charge. "You gentlemen here for the show?"

"Sure are. We're her escorts." John replied, deadpan, his hand on Kenzie's shoulder, and the others laughed. The bouncer shrugged.

"It's your money." He said and let them pass. The interior was pretty much what Kenzie expected—a bar pretending to be someone's idea of a house of ill repute. The stage extended into the middle of the building, with tables lining the floor all around it.

There were a lot more women in the audience than she had expected. In fact, Kenzie looked around suspiciously; the audience was almost all female. Apparently, strip shows had changed since she was an adventurous college senior and had gone to a club with her male friends. Then she had been the only woman with all her clothes on.

The arrival of seven mostly young, muscular, and generally good-looking men brought a swirl of activity around their table. Rather like throwing chum into shark-infested waters, Kenzie thought, as one woman draped herself around John, much to his discomfort and Kenzie's amusement. She only hoped the feeding frenzy would leave her unscathed. A scantily clad waitress with bored eyes served drinks around the table, and the men unmercifully harassed the rookie. The lights went down even farther, blurring the dubious décor. Blinding strobe lights started flashing in time with raucous rock and roll. The emcee stepped on stage.

"And now, ladies, and of course our gentlemen," He nodded towards the seven firefighters, "The Lucky Lady is proud to bring you, for the first time ever, our new all-male review. Are you ready for a bumpy ride?" He stepped off stage to the screams of two hundred women. Kenzie's shriek of laughter was drowned in driving music. The looks on the faces of her brother firefighters were priceless. Kenzie would have given anything for a camera. Revenge, even unplanned, was exquisite. She settled in to enjoy the show, ignoring the furious debate going on at her table.

Four male dancers, hair spiked to fine points, muscled and showing tantalizing hints of bronzed skin, yet dressed in full clothing, came out on stage. They stripped off one item at a time to the driving beat and flashing strobes, interspersing the stripping with moves more suited to the bedroom or a porn movie than the stage. Kenzie was torn between laughter and shock. By the time the dancers were down to their whitey-tighties, and tight they definitely were, Kenzie was on her feet, cheering as loudly as the other women.

"Kenzie. Hey. We are going across the road to the other strip club. Let's go." John leaned over and yelled in her ear.

"You have got to be kidding. This is much better than a bunch of women getting naked. Go on. I'll catch up with you later."

"Be careful. This is a bad neighborhood."

"Gee, where a strip club is? Go figure."

"I'm serious. I'll come to get you after the show. You wait here until I come to get you." He looked around at the screaming women. "These women sound like they'd eat their young."

"Only their husbands. Or the dancers. Or you. Go on. You'll be a whole lot safer." The others filed out, and Kenzie's table, in a prime spot, soon filled with other women. One of the dancers came down into the audience and selected a giggling and willing prop. She was staged on a couch on the stage while the dancer performed around her. It was an eye raising dance and brought the audience to a, Kenzie sniggered as the thought occurred to her, universal climax.

The five dancers leaped off the stage, and the women held up money. In exchange for bills stuffed in G-strings, the women participated in their very own very definitely un-private lap dances. Kenzie watched in disbelief as one dancer stuffed a bill down a woman's shirt and then removed it with his teeth. This was definitely not what she expected. As she stared in surprise and, well, a splash of prurience, the male dancer gave her a luscious wink and a suggestive lip lick. Kenzie felt her eyebrows crawl to new heights.

The dancers headed backstage, and a new duo came out. Kenzie vaguely realized one was singing in the background while the other performed a romantic; if that was the right word for it, strip for some lucky lady he had brought on stage. The singer was outstanding, and she wished she could hear him better. In fact, he sounded somewhat familiar. Kenzie frowned. Not everything had to remind her of Lee. Tonight, she would enjoy the spectacle; tomorrow, she could go back to fretting.

The singer started in with another song, one she recognized instantly and with great rue. It was Old Blue Eyes himself. She rather thought he had never imagined such use for his anthem to independence. And, she had to admit, the dancers were certainly doing it their way. It took a relatively large amount of muscle to hold the poses the dancers were in and undulate in such a fashion. There were a couple of poses she thought might be useful if she ever got around to that sort of fun again, but a few were pretty impossible for a couple. Kenzie shook her head to relieve the pornographic pictures parading all dressed in whitey-tighties through her brain.

Her newly discovered favorite dancer was out on the catwalk, doing a solo, Kenzie fanned her face, and the singer beat out a hard-rocking anthem to drugs and sex. There was a pause, and again all the dancers came off the stage for more un-private dancing. Kenzie shrugged. What was good for the gander was good for the goose, although she had never heard of female strippers performing in quite this manner. She pulled a bill from her pocket and held it up, looking around to see who was closest.

A warm, sweaty body collided with her, and he turned, teeth flashing in a welcoming smile, hand reaching for the bill. Their eyes met, and Kenzie froze, a Zen moment smashing her over the head. The dancer's eyes widened in absolute horror, and he spun away while dozens of women surging between them. He was trying to move away from her, but the women blocked his way, screaming for dances. And, with a grin and shrug, he complied.

It was even more disturbing than the previous dances. Somehow more suggestive. Infinitely pornographic. And entirely too familiar. Their eyes met, the dancer taking malicious delight in her discomfort. Kenzie staggered down onto her seat. She sat very still for a few moments, not hearing the roar of the crowd or music, very carefully, not looking at anything. Only her heartbeat pounding loudly, accompanied by swirling dizziness. Masochism drew her eyes back up, but the dancer was gone. She wondered briefly if throwing up would make her feel better.

She stood and forced her way past bodies swaying to the music, past the bouncers and servers, and into the cool night air. She staggered a little, sucking in deep breaths of if not precisely clean air, at least not contaminated with the pheromones of two hundred hot and bothered women. Great, now any cop watching the place would pull her over for DUI.

She walked down the parking lot, going up the first row, looking for a specific vehicle. She found it, four cars over and one row up, near the stage door in the darkest part of the parking lot. There it was Lee's truck with its out-of-state license plates with the same state as hers. She went to her SUV and tried to think.

Getting in her car was an invitation to a DUI ticket, and she really did not want to cross the busy highway on foot to get to the motel. Not to mention that JohnB would have kittens if he came back and she was gone. Kenzie went back to the truck and sat against the bumper. Probably not the best neighborhood to sit outside a strip club in the dark.

"Enough." Kenzie snarled, walked back to the pickup, and plunked down on the bumper. Bring'em on, baby. She could use a good outlet for this raging surge of embarrassment and anger. She leaned her head back against the truck cap.

The nights he was gone and refused to tell her where. So, Lee had been stripping in clubs, not burning down buildings. Who'd-a thunk it, Kenzie groaned to herself. At least, arson was marginally more respectable. Of all the things he could have been doing, this was one that certainly had never occurred to her.

Kenzie was not sure if she was more stunned by the concrete example of why Lee had had a gym bag full of black clothing or by the thought of him sashaying around in his mostly all together. His mother and father would surely be surprised. Lay an egg was a more polite form of the response that occurred to her. She giggled a little hysterically and wiped away a few tears. It was a very long time to wait, and her thoughts surged in confusing eddies, not letting her dwell too long on any one thought.

Eventually, the show ended. From the snippets of conversation Kenzie overheard, there was still dancing going on, but the show itself was over. Later, the last of the women surged out in a laughing, drunken crowd. Kenzie waited. In a relatively short time, the women were gone, and the parking lot was nearly empty when he came out, swinging the black gym bag by one handle. Kenzie felt her stomach drop into her shoes. Now that she knew what she was seeing, his gracefulness was unmistakably that of a dancer. She closed her eyes to muster inner strength, and when she opened them, he was watching her warily.

"Hey." Kenzie managed.

"Get off my truck. You'll scratch the paint." Lee snapped. Kenzie stood up. "What do you want?"

"To talk to you."

"I got nothing to say to you."

"I... I thought you were fantastic tonight." A long silence. "Worth every dollar those women stuffed in your G-string." The snide comment slipped out before she could censor it.

"Noticed you didn't," Lee responded with a derisive grin. Kenzie gritted her teeth. The conversation was not going the way she imagined it would.

"Why should I pay for what I had for free?" Kenzie returned, shocked at herself. For a second, she thought he was going to hit her. This conversation was really not going well, and it was going downhill fast.

"Maybe you should have. I certainly had to pay for it."

"Fine." She took out a dollar and stuffed it down the front of his shirt. Lee's hand came up to block the motion but chose instead to take the dollar out of his shirt and crumple it. He raised his fist between them and dropped the dollar to the ground in a gesture of absolute contempt. They glared at each other like alley cats before Kenzie snorted in disgust and turned toward her SUV.

"What in the hell are you doing here, anyway?" Lee asked.

"I came down with JohnB and some other guys." Kenzie

turned back. "They went to the strip club across the street when they found out about the...um.... all-male review."

"Thank god for small favors." He unlocked his truck and tossed his bag in. "Is there something else?"

"No. Not really." Kenzie replied. Lee stepped up on the running board of his truck, ready to get in and drive off. Kenzie mentally kicked herself. Now or never. "Why didn't you tell me? About this?" She could not quite bring herself to say stripping, waving her hand in the direction of the Lucky Ladies. Lee stepped back down, and for the briefest moment, Kenzie thought she saw a sadness in his eyes.

"What difference would it have made?"

"A lot. Geez, my boyfriend took his clothes off for a bunch of women and then dirty danced with them. I'm not really sure how I feel about that little detail you omitted from our relationship."

"Good reason not to tell you."

"It took you three months to work up the nerve to kiss me."

"Was it nerve or desire?" Lee snapped. Kenzie settled in for a good fight.

"Nerve or desire, it made no difference at the time, did it?"

"Maybe I was just making sure you were the type of woman who didn't get her jollies at strip shows."

"Well, I certainly didn't get my jollies tonight. That was really creepy, seeing my ex up there strutting in his G-string. Not to mention prostituting himself for a bunch of horny women."

"I'm not your ex. That's one title I surely do not want. And I'm a singer. Not a dancer."

"Really. You could have fooled me tonight. The line was a tad bit blurred, near as I could tell. And don't worry. Your secret is safe with me. I have no desire for my brother firefighters to find out about your extra-curricular activities. I'd never live it down."

"And you've lived down turning me in as an arsonist? Last I heard, you are toxic waste." Lee scored the final point. Kenzie admitted it to herself and looked down to hide the hurt and shame his last remark had stung into showing. At least he was talking to her, even if he was not making it easy.

Kenzie rubbed her head, a nasty headache starting from the tension. She wanted to mutter not very ladylike imprecations under her breath to calm her nerves, but the one she would be calling names was herself.

"If I had known, maybe things would have turned out differently. You could have told me where you were when the fires started. Instead of just gone."

"You could have trusted me." His words hung in the air between them and Kenzie wondered if he had the grace to blush.

"Yeah, well. There's the rub. For what it's worth, I'm glad it wasn't you. And I'm sorry."

"You should be," Lee said softly. Kenzie shook her head and walked away. Time to let it go. They had both said some nasty things, and it was time to end it.

"Why'd you do it?" Lee's voice was directly behind her, and she spun around. He was very close to her, and she felt a fission of fear. She had forgotten how much space he could take up when he was in cop mode.

"I told you. The night you left. Every fire started on a night you were gone. I left a book in your truck. When I went to find it, I found a box full of the same incendiary devices the arsonist used. And then I found your duffle bag, and since I didn't know you were prancing about taking off your clothes for a bunch of strange women, it appeared to me that there were a whole lot of coincidences that could be easily explained by you being the arsonist."

"I still can't believe you thought it was me."

"Well, I did, and frankly, if you'd said something, anything, this might not ever have happened." Kenzie paused, "Course, I'm not sure how I'd feel about the whole stripping thing."

"Singing, not stripping."

"Whatever. Why are you so secretive?"

"Do you have any idea how much grief I'd catch if my fellow officers found out? I'd be laughed out of the service."

"Then, why do it?"

Lee shrugged. "It's fun. I've done it for a lot of years. I make lots of spending money. Gives me something to do. Instead of setting fires. At least for a few more years. You women don't like looking at us older guys."

"And that's different from guys.... How?" Kenzie snapped. The silence stretched long between them.

"I went over the data six ways to Sunday, trying to disprove it was you, by the way, with Bob Chu and the ATF," Kenzie said softly. The closest she could come to apologizing.

"He told me about that."

"Bob did?" Kenzie asked. Lee nodded. "That was nice of him."

"I think he was trying to keep me from adding assault to my list of sins."

"Oh."

"How about your TV buddy as arsonist?"

"Gordo? We've looked into him as well. He never has an alibi, he's always around, but he is legitimately everywhere on news business. I think he lives for news; he certainly doesn't do anything else. He's also been accommodating, taking crowd shots. The fires flare up so sporadically, we can't find a motive. The coincidences were a lot stronger in your... favor." Kenzie's words fell over themselves in her eagerness for Lee to understand. "I just don't understand the candles. Even now that I know why you are running around with masks in your gym bag, I don't understand the candles."

"Come on, Kenzie. You have as many of those damned things as I do."

"Not scooped out of the holders. Not rolling around the back of my SUV." Kenzie argued back.

"Oh, for the love of... How many times do I have to tell you it wasn't me?"

"Why were the candles in your truck?" Kenzie looked up into Lee's brown eyes. So close, but the distance between them had never been greater. She knew every plane of his face; the way light made his eyes turn dark green, and what made them dance with laughter, and she had missed him so much. Right now, his eyes glittered with rage, and he was suddenly entirely too close to her.

"I. Am. Not. Your. Arsonist. I am about two seconds away from reporting you for harassment. And unlike me, you are guilty of the charge. Now, go away." Lee's voice was flat. Kenzie stood for a moment, just looking at him. She had missed him more than she cared to admit.

"I'd imagine the guys will be heading back, or at least John will. If you don't want him to see you, you better go." Kenzie said quietly. Lee turned without another word and got into his truck. He pulled past her and stopped.

"Go get in your SUV, Kenz. This is a bad neighborhood." He rolled back up his window and drove off. Kenzie watched him go. He did not look back.

"Hey, Kenz. Make a new friend?" JohnB popped out of the shadows.

"No, just talking to one of the... singers. Show over?"

"More or less. I've had enough of looky no touchy. Ready for bed? Or do you want something to drink?"

"Shower and bed. I feel a little dirty." Kenzie said quietly. JohnB put his arm around her and walked her back to her SUV, where Flower waited patiently.

It would be a long time before she saw Lee again.

Kenzie parked her SUV in the station parking lot and let Flower out. She looked curiously at the other cars in the lot. There were more than could be accounted for by the regular shift workers. Hopefully, the chief had not called a surprise meeting. She was hoping to do something outside today; the weather was gloriously cool for August but with a hint of the heat to come later in the day. A meeting would eat up all the cool time.

The side bay door tended to stick, and Kenzie yanked on it. As it came open, a snake arrowed towards her, moving at unbelievable speed. Kenzie shrieked and slammed the door shut, leaning on it as if to keep the snake from opening the door. Her heart was pounding, and she could even feel it in her ears. Flower barked his deep, intruder alert bark. Kenzie pushed herself off the door and hushed Flower. In the sudden silence, she could hear waves of laughter coming from the bay.

Cautiously, Kenzie opened the door a crack and peered around it. The snake lay still in the middle of the floor, and she could see the light reflecting off a fishing line strung from the snake to the door handle. Across the bay was a video camera on a tripod, the recording light glowing red. For a brief second, thoughts of violence flashed through her mind. This was, after all, the fire service, where practical jokes were the norm. Plus, she would do the same, given the proper circumstances. Revenge would be carefully thought out and served very cold.

Kenzie took a deep breath and steeled her shaking legs. As she crossed the bay, Flower growled at the very dead snake and made a large detour around it, his tail tucked between his legs and ruff standing on end. Pulling the door open to the station kitchen, she found the entire previous day's shift and most of her shift waiting. They leaped to their feet, shrieking in parody.

"Ooo, a snake."

"Oh, my stars and garters."

"Help!!" Kenzie could not help but join in the laughter. Someone hurried out to reset the snake.

"Quiet, everyone. JohnB just pulled in." The other John called from the entry. Kenzie took a place where she could see into the bay. JohnB hated snakes and always had, but Kenzie was pretty certain he had never told his brother firefighters about his phobia. Kenzie had found out entirely by accident.

If anything, JohnB's scream was even louder than hers, Kenzie thought with satisfaction. He slammed the door so hard that it bounced back, and the snake shot almost through the doorway. The door did not open for a very long time, and when it did, he was armed with a large stick. Kenzie could see his knuckles were white as he gripped the stick. He prodded the snake a few times and tossed his stick into the garbage can near the bay doors. The chief sat with his head on the table, shoulders shaking. Another howled and snorted. Another leaned on the sink and laughed, legs refusing to hold him up. The camaraderie and esprit de corps were almost visible in the room.

"I'm going to have to change my uniform. You idiots." JohnB laughed. He played tricks on everyone and was the first to appreciate a good one played on him.

"We thought you were going to run to the next county." Cap laughed.

"I hope you got that on video." John Two gingerly pulled the snake along the floor, and the crew waited for the next victim.

After the last man came in and the previous day's crew left, Kenzie's crew disposed of the snake and settled down to work.

"Where'd the snake come from?" JohnB asked.

"Kermit found it when he was fishing Sunday," Kurt answered.

"He killed it?" Kenzie asked in disbelief. Kermit released flies from inside the station rather than to squish them. The fire station's general consensus was that Kermit's fishing habit was a cover for ogling girls on the lake. Never once had they heard he had actually caught a fish.

"Yeah, right. It was already dead."

Revenge would be his. Fire spoke to him in the depths of his heart and told him how to avenge all the fires that died at the hands of the firefighters. He could no longer control the need to burn and the pressure behind his eyes, deep in his brain, had to be appeased. His hands shook, and he emptied another candleholder and laid the rags out so that it would pull the fire away from the candle and into the trash piled high in this basement. The floor was ready. Now for the bait. He lit the candle and crept up the stairs to start the smaller fire well across the floor. Fire would speak tonight, and its voice would never be silenced. Tonight, Kenzie would regret her every decision, from deciding to be a firefighter to trying to crush him into oblivion. She would pay. He struck the match and lit the wick.

He backed out carefully and closed the door on the future inferno. His bike was waiting, and he calmly biked away.

Chapter 12

Despite the snake incident, it turned out to be a tranquil day, but Kenzie felt a vague creeping sense of urgency. The feeling seemed to pervade the rest of her station mates, and tempers were short. They all knew the arsons had happened on quiet days as if someone was trying to add unwanted excitement to their lives. On top of that, it had been an exceedingly long time. It was more than a year since the arsonist had set anything ablaze. Since Lee's investigation, Kenzie thought to herself. Most arsonists could not contain their need for fire, and this delay was adding to his rage and power lust. His next fire would probably be horrible, as if to make up for the hiatus.

When the tone went off, announcing a house fire, Kenzie's anxiety increased. A spontaneous house fire was dangerous enough, but when fires started with malice aforethought, the fires were much more dangerous. Arsonists were perfectly capable of sabotaging a structure, and more than one firefighter had died at the hand of an arsonist. She climbed into the cab next to JohnB. He grinned at her, eyes alight with the excitement of facing down his enemy. Kenzie liked the firefighter life. JohnB lived for it.

This house was on the city's edge, half the property inside

the city and half outside. The old owner had been eccentric and had fought efforts to incorporate. He stated that he and his had been there before the city and would be there after the city was gone. As it turned out, he was wrong. He had died with no heirs, and the property was tied up in court. It had been vacant for a long time, and Kenzie did not relish going inside with who knew what structural damage. The windows were boarded up, and the porch had a definite slant to it.

County would be arriving soon to help. Kenzie swung out of the cab, pulling on her helmet. She glanced around, a habit now that she was looking for the arsonist. Lee stood beside his patrol car on the edge of the fire scene. Their eyes met, and she felt a shock deep in her stomach. He had every reason to be here, she reminded herself. This was city land as well. She forgot to buckle her helmet in the breaking of routine.

"You need to catch the arsonist, Kenzie." JohnB bumped into her, breaking her paralysis.

"I tried, dammit."

"Stevenson, Barstow. You take a hose in the front door. Smith, Curtis. Go in the side. Chris, you're on back up. Kurt, you too, after you pull the plywood off the windows." Cap called out orders, and the fire scene exploded with activity.

Kenzie and JohnB hauled hose to the front door and dropped to their knees. JohnB shoved the door open. Smoke billowed out, but from deep within, she could see the unblinking ruby glow of a scorching hot fire across the room from them. If she had to guess in the gloom, they were headed for the kitchen. Kenzie waited to feel the hose surge under her gloved hands, but JohnB held off turning the nozzle on. They crawled across towards the burning room.

Kenzie caught the flash of reflective tape in the kitchen

and then the thick smoke of a dying fire. Another group of firefighters had entered the room and were putting water on the fire. There was an odd whoosh, and the fire exploded into wild flames. Everywhere water went, the fire followed. There was no question now that this fire had been set. JohnB glanced back at her, his eyes wide behind his mask. Her brain flicked through all the accelerants that reacted acutely with water.

JohnB jerked his hose up towards the ceiling to cool the gases trapped there and prevent flashover. Flashovers occurred when gases, given off by normal combustion, collected and heated to the point when they spontaneously and instantly caught on fire. In that event, the fire would swim on the ceiling, drip down the walls, and roast anything under it. It was a firefighter's nightmare.

This was worse. The arsonist had used something that reacted with water in his fire. She hoped the other team was backing out to get for the foam extinguishers. JohnB turned off the hose and began to turn toward her. That much she could feel in the gloom. She began to back up, pulling the hose with her. Without warning, the hose lifted up in her hands, nozzle whistling past her head. It pulled her almost to her feet and then fell, writhing like a snake, then bucking like a horse. She fought the hose as water pressure made it dance and whip with a life of its own.

Kenzie threw herself flat onto the hose, holding it still with her body weight, and peered around, reaching out along the floor with one hand to find JohnB. Only empty air met her hand, and her heart contracted in terror. Whatever was wrong was very wrong. JohnB would never abandon her to the beast. The nozzle whistled past her head, and she grabbed for it, missing in the gloom. It came back with a vengeance, knocking the hose into her head. Her helmet tilted sideways, hanging off her facemask. Kenzie dropped her head down and inched farther up the hose toward the nozzle. Then there was nothing beneath her as the floor gave way. She fell headfirst into fire and darkness, into hell. Her helmet hit on something and went spiraling off below her.

Kenzie heard herself whimper as she caught herself on the hose and then almost lost her grip as the rest of her body fell past her hands. Kenzie wrapped her legs around the hose and held on. Below her was an inferno of flames, smoke, and glowing red spots that looked like demon's eyes. She pressed her face against the hose to hold on her facemask and air hose in place, even just for her own peace of mind. Just for a brief, frantic moment, she felt the mask suck into her face, and she remembered the feeling of her air pack running empty. Her lungs could drag in nothing.

No! Kenzie stomped hard on the incipient panic. Her mask was not too tight, no alarm screamed in her ear; there was still air in her pack. Breathe slowly, shallowly. Trust her equipment. Trust her brother firefighters. Where the Nomex hood had been pulled out of place when her helmet had ripped off, she could feel the exposed flesh burning. Her weight stilled the hose above her, but the nozzle still whipped under her. She slipped a little farther, and one foot found a precarious hold on the nozzle handle. Water sprayed the fire, making the smoke worse. She concentrated on breathing, holding a count of four. She let her breath out slowly and held onto the hose. Her world narrowed to those concerns. Dimly, she heard her PSD began shrieking its warning to her brother firefighters.

She stared in cross-eyed amazement as her mask began to bubble. The words of her rookie school instructor played in her ears. A bubbling mask was an awful sign. Trust your equipment, the same voice said. She gripped even more tightly, trusting to Nomex. It was hot. Too hot. If she let go, she would join JohnB down in the belly of the dragon. Water cascaded down over her and stopped the burning.

An eternity later, the hose began to move upward. Hands grabbed her by anything they could reach and pulled her onto the floor. Two firefighters grabbed her by the shoulder straps of her air pack and dragged her out of the house, shoulders first. She could see the fire raging behind her, the brilliant red showing through the thick black smoke.

The paramedics met them at the doorway, dragging her the rest of the way to the engine, to safety. Her boots bounced across the wet ground, leaving drag marks. She could not take her eyes off the house and the firefighters who were now racing against terrible odds to save one of their own. Hands pulled off her facemask and Nomex hood.

"John's still in there. He went through the floor." Kenzie croaked. The pain was incredible.

"They're trying to get him out now." One of county's paramedics held her down as she struggled to get up.

"Let me go. I need a fresh air pack and a new face mask and helmet." Kenzie insisted. The medic shoved her down. Kenzie managed to get one knee under her. She shoved up against the hands that were between her and the fire. The other medic fell backward, and Kenzie surged up. There was extra gear in the engine.

"Don't be stupid, Kenzie." A familiar voice snapped at her, one of her own medics. She swung around on him in anger and bewilderment.

"Let me borrow your face mask and helmet." She snapped

at Chris Malone. The other medic scrambled to his feet.

"Jesus, Kenzie, sit down and shut up." The two men forced her down beside the rescue truck and shoved an oxygen mask over her face. Kenzie ripped it off.

"Let me go." Kenzie shrieked. Another body joined the fray, holding her down.

"Kenzie, sit down and let the medics work on you." An unexpected voice said in her ear, and hands on her face forced her head around. Lee's dark brown eyes met hers, compassion brimming in them.

"John's in there. I have to get him out." Kenzie looked up at Lee. In her shock, she could not remember why Lee should not be at the fire. She only knew she was glad to see him.

"They're doing all they can. You need to let the other firefighters do their job and let the medics do theirs." Lee knelt down beside her, putting one arm around her.

"It's my job. JohnB's my partner." Kenzie insisted. Someone else was pulling off her coat and wrapping a blood pressure cuff around her arm. She did not understand why they were not getting John out. Someone smeared something cool on her face, and she realized how badly her face hurt. Every time she tried to get up, Lee's hands forced her back down. Emotional shock and adrenaline-fueled terror had erased thought, and she was running on instinct.

"Let's go, Kenzie. The ambulance is here." Chris looked down at her. Kenzie held onto Lee's shirt, shrinking into him.

"No, not until John comes out. We can ride in together." Kenzie said, her eyes glued back to the fire. The men looked at each other. Chris rubbed a fist viciously across his face leaving smears of water to glisten in the firelight.

"Is Kenzie in any danger?" Lee asked. Chris shook his head,

and the other medic answered for him.

"No, second degree burns, no shock... yet. She needs to get to the hospital for a complete checkup, you know, airway burns, that sort of thing but..."

"Let her wait, please," Lee asked. The medics frowned at each other, sending silent messages between themselves. They looked back down at him.

"Aren't you..." Chris' voice was deep with suspicion.

"Yes," Lee answered shortly.

"If you started this, I'll kill you myself." Anger shook the medic's voice.

"Fine." Lee snapped, "Knock yourself out, but I'm not your main concern right now. Kenzie is. I can keep her calm if you shut up." Anger made his voice crack like a whip. He could see the other men taking offense. He took a deep breath, deepened his voice to the timber that upset people respected. "Let her wait for John. For whatever..." Lee calmed his voice, offering conciliation. Chris glanced at Kenzie, who was leaning against Lee.

"Fine." Chris unconsciously mimicked Lee and then walked away. Kenzie leaned her head against Lee's shoulder, drawing what comfort she could as they watched the house burn.

More engines arrived, along with the media. A firefighter down was big news and made for great evening news coverage. Two crews fought the fire back with foam while the others concentrated on reaching JohnB in the basement. Deep in her heart, Kenzie knew it was too late for John, but until the final curtain, she would hold out hope for him.

The basement had been a trap. Kenzie knew that as wholly and suddenly as if she had set it herself. Someone had built a super-hot fire in the basement with a decoy fire on the main floor to draw them in across the floor. The fire in the basement would have killed John long before the air in his pack ran out if the fall had not mercifully killed him. However, she could hope.

The fire was all but out when they brought him up. The fire had been so hot that there was almost nothing left. Nomex melted, canvas burned, and it was all massed together in a char of what had been their companion. They had paused, inside the door, to put what remained in a body bag, and then four, one at each corner, carried it out in a spontaneous honor guard. All around, firefighters stood or knelt, watching and praying. JohnB's station mates were crying openly, the other crews silent.

Kenzie hid her face from the sight of the body bag, clutching Lee's shirt, oblivious to the pain of the burns on her face. Tears poured down her face, soaking into his shirt. Lee rested his face against her hair, drawing in a shuddering breath. Not only had John been his friend, but it was only luck that Kenzie was not coming out in the same condition. His arms tightened around her. One of the medics came back to check on Kenzie.

"I... John." Words failed her as she tried to express her grief.

"Oh, God. He's gone." Chris, the medic, wiped away a tear. "Dammit, Kenzie. That's why we don't want women on the fire line. What'd you do to screw up in there? John shouldn't have died because of you."

Kenzie cringed into Lee, who took in a furious breath.

"That's enough, Malone." Cap's deep voice rumbled over their heads. "You have a patient. Take care of her." He knelt in front of Kenzie and gently took her face in one big hand, forcing her to look at him and not at the activity around the fire scene. "Looks like that hurts. What happened?" His voice was gentle and non-accusatory. Kenzie squeezed her eyes shut, marshaling self-control. When she opened them, she was able to speak calmly.

"I was behind... him on the hose. When the other crew hit the fire in the back of the house, the fire exploded. J... we started to back out. To get foam. He was gone. Then the floor gave way, and I had hold of the hose, and I didn't let go..." She recited the facts carefully, voice small. Shudders wracked her body. "I'm sorry about my helmet. And my faceplate melting."

"It's okay, Kenzie. You did fine." His voice was quiet. He looked up at the upset medic. "She's going into shock. Get her in that damned ambulance and get her the hell out of here." He rumbled off, and Kenzie looked up at Lee.

"I'm so sorry, Kenzie." His voice was gentle. She buried her face in his shirt and bawled. Lee held her, rocking slowly back and forth until the medics came with the stretcher to take her to the ambulance.

The picture was perfect. Kenzie sat in the protective circle of Lee's arms. Fire glistened off the tear tracks on her face and lit the scene with an eerie light. Lee had his forehead resting on Kenzie's head. Another firefighter ran out of the scene, caught in the air between strides. Gordo stared in wonder at his masterpiece. This was it, Pulitzer Prize and fame. He had done it at long last. The wire services would pick up the picture, and it would be flashed all over the globe, and on television, his picture would move people to tears. This picture was worth everything, every effort, every sacrifice. Even John's. Or maybe especially John Barstow's. Being there with his digital camera instead of the video camera had been a stroke of genius.

The pungent smell of perfume announced Tina's presence in

the newsroom. The TV personalities did not often come into the print side of the news partnership. Gordo was one of the few who crossed the lines, freelancing for both organizations. Tina was happy. Gordo cringed. His infatuation with her had faded, and instead, he was very, very frightened of her, especially in this mood. How could something so lovely be so very awful, he wondered.

"What do you have there?" Her voice was playful, and she was all smiles. The other reporters were suitably sobered by the evening events. Many had known John Barstow, and while his death would sell papers, the reporters still felt terrible.

"Nothing," Gordo mumbled.

"Let me see it." Tina took the picture out of his hands. Gordo watched the changes come over her face. The smiles fled, followed by that scary calm Gordo had learned to fear. Mindlessly, she crumbled the photo in her hands, knuckles turning white. Gordo whimpered in protest. Tina dropped the photo on the floor and turned on one heel, stalking out of the newsroom doors.

Gordo retrieved his masterpiece, smoothing out the wrinkles and hating Tina. He could print more, the digital image would live on, but this, his masterpiece, was ruined. Gordo sat silently, hoping she was gone. It was very conceivable that she could rage back through like a hurricane. Silence reigned as the reporters eyed him curiously and cautiously. At least while she was gone, he felt more confident. He could admire his work in solitude.

The death had shaken him badly. He had meant for someone to die, but the reality of it had been almost too much. On the one hand, his plans had worked perfectly, and he could hardly believe his luck.

JohnB had come between him and Kenzie and had deserved to die. Fire had said he was the murderer of the little fires he had set to honor Fire. He hated John Barstow, and now he was dead, painfully and in terror. And Kenzie was crushed. Fire had spoken, and it had won, showing the world that it was not tamed, and by extension, he was more powerful than they were. Finally, and forever. He did not need to start another fire. This last one was enough.

Chapter 13

Kenzie was finally alone in her hospital room. They were keeping her overnight, just to make sure she was all right. She knew she would never be all right again. She had not been able to answer the doctor's questions without crying. Then she had had to endure a continual stream of visitors in the form of the chief, the chaplain, her station captain, and a couple of firefighters. Lee had been there as well, lurking in the background, but he had gone back to the fire station to get Flower and take him home. Nothing made sense anymore.

The occasional creak of nurses' shoes in the hallway outside her door made her feel secure. She rolled over onto her side, facing away from the door and the light leaking around the edges. She closed her eyes and watched John laugh heartily over the dead snake in the bay only that morning, saw his anger at the pointless deaths he had seen over the years on medical calls, followed him through the years they had been enemies and then friends.

She had always wanted to be a firefighter, but her father, as steeped in the life as anyone, had vetoed it. That was not the life he wanted for his little girl. If she wanted to join the fire service, Kenzie should join as a paramedic, not as a line firefighter. She had listened, toddling off to college to major in something, spending summer with a red card putting out range fires for the BLM. Then two things had happened. The first was Introduction to Criminal Justice, taught by Doc James. The other was an ad for open testing at the local station.

She had been the only woman at the testing, and she sat alone at a table, the first taste of what was to come. The test was easy enough, she thought. She had spent her life with the terminology and working on the wildfire line. The knowledge testing was where she first saw JohnB, leaning up against a wall to proctor the exam. Every time she glanced up, he was watching her as if he expected her to whip out an answer sheet and crib from it.

Once back on campus, she waited in agonized silence until the letter came. Kenzie ripped open the envelope in the college post office, shouting with glee as she read the results. Second out of everyone who had tested. An invitation to the physical testing, a variation on the firefighter challenge, to test her agility and stamina followed.

There were five slots with forty candidates waiting to fill them. Kenzie mentally grouped her fellow hopefuls. The lone girl. The ex-military— they were the ones with short hair standing at aggressive parade rest. The wannabes, some volunteer firefighters, some red cardholders. And the real thing. Standing in a cluster well away from the trainees, the career firefighters watched their potential future comrades. From this point on, each candidate was in an interview without questions. Their every action would be witnessed and commented on. Butterflies clogged up her stomach, and Kenzie wished she had not had her morning coffee since a bathroom break was not forthcoming.

The test included dragging one hundred fifty-pound dummies; climbing ladders to the top of the training tower and making her way back down the unlit stairwell; hauling the hose up to the top of the tower, carrying a hose roll along a balance beam, and running. Because she was a female, Kenzie got extra time to complete her tasks, but it was her goal to make at least the bottom of the men's time limits, a challenge she met quite handily. Overall, she had tested so well that the fire department had no choice but to offer her a job or face a lawsuit. Next, there was rookie school to get through, and that, her father shook his head over. In this most masculine of careers, a woman had an uphill fight and, possible legal action notwithstanding, Kenzie would get no breaks.

JohnB was one of the trainers for rookie school. His job was to challenge, to teach, and make sure the rookies did not kill themselves or someone else. However, in Kenzie's eyes, he had another mission, to make her wash out. Everywhere she was, he was right behind her, sighing exaggeratedly if she did not do something quite right and grudgingly showing her the correct way. Or giving her the gimlet eye when explaining their potential screw-ups as if she would be the only one to commit the errors. Kenzie kept her expression bland, but the constant sub-level harassment eroded her confidence.

Like dogs who take their cues from, and obey only the alpha male, the rest of the trainees avoided her. Her lunches were eaten in virtual solitary with an invisible cootie line, as Kenzie thought of it, clearly drawn around her. She studied alone. No one wanted to be her partner. Now that she was trying for a career job in the real world, she indulged herself in a bit of revenge fantasy. In her apartment, off-campus, she fantasized about standing up in the middle of the room and screaming obscenities before blasting everyone with either fire or water. Her daydreams varied depending on how obnoxious JohnB had been. He had even slapped her with her nickname, Fire Chick, and it was not meant in the nicest possible way at all.

Kenzie hung a picture of the first professional woman firefighter up in her room and reminded herself that she was breaking a new trail, and if she washed out, so would a generation of women after her. She hated JohnB with a deep and abiding passion.

She passed rookie school and looked forward to her next assignment, one of the stations far away from JohnB. She just could not stand it if she was crewed with him.

And as luck or perversity would have it, she was. Sitting next to John in the jump seat, behind him on the line. Someone either had a wicked sense of humor, or more likely, someone wanted her gone. Kenzie set her teeth and went to work. Some of the harassment was doled out in equal measure. Rookies were rookies, regardless of gender.

JohnB had insisted she cook a meal. Kenzie prepared the worst possible dinner she could think of. There was no way she would be stuck in the role of fire department cook just because she was the little woman. He had insisted on her scrubbing out the equipment boxes. She had complied with goodwill, even when he had found a molecule of dirt and made her do it again. She had redone it, happy movies of torture and pain playing in her brain as she scrubbed spotless metal again.

The entire crew would be laughing until she sat down to lunch or dinner, at which point the whole crew would clam up. She recognized it as possible shyness or the intrusion of female on male lack of manners and presence of crude, possibly inappropriate humor. Kenzie bore it with as good grace as she possibly could. Her father kept his opinions to himself, a trait that endeared him to her.

She had been serving for almost a full year when the call had come in for a trailer fire, smoke showing. The trailer was puffing smoke out various holes in its construction, and JohnB was sent in with Kenzie on hose to attack the fire from inside. "Come on, Chickie." He grinned at her. It was the first truly pleasant expression she had seen on his face when he had dealt with her. However, she had recognized it as the joy of confronting the beast in its lair, not of genuine camaraderie. In her memory, Kenzie could see his face, shining in the firelight, knight of fire, and she choked back a sob.

They had crept towards the back bedroom. House trailers were nasty places to fight a fire. Built of pressboard and glue, they burned like tissue paper and collapsed when wet. This one was no exception. As they edged down the hall towards the fire, the floor under JohnB's feet gave way, and he fell the five feet to the ground below, taking Kenzie with him. Like a good firefighter, he kept control of the hose. Kenzie bounced off him grunting as she collided with his air pack. She groaned as she rubbed at the future bruises. JohnB rolled his eyes at her.

"Shit." JohnB tried to hoist himself up to the main floor, but his weight crumbled the floor. "Come're, rookie. Go put the wet stuff on the red stuff." Effortlessly, he hoisted her out of the hole, onto solid flooring, and handed her the hose. Kenzie crept on to the fire and learned the joy of fighting fire. She had laughed soundlessly in her mask: I am woman, hear me roar. JohnB and all his nastiness would never make her give in or quit.

The fire out; smoke vented out the broken windows. Kenzie glanced around the room. A mass of melted glass with a fused mass of metal on top of it seemed to be the ignition point. An aquarium? The denizens were fried fish by now if so. She headed back down the hall. All she could see of JohnB was his head and shoulders, and his eyes were very, very large behind his air mask.

"Want up, or would you rather crawl out past all the spiders?" Kenzie pulled her facemask off and clipped it to her harness, careful to put her helmet back on. JohnB did not move.

"I'm not alone down here, Rook... er.... Kenzie." His voice shook. "There's something... crawling up my legs." His voice squeaked on the word something. Kenzie whipped out her flashlight and shined it down the hole. Two glittery eyes stared back. Kenzie cursed and scuttled back.

"How do you feel about really large snakes?" Kenzie asked. JohnB jumped and then yelped.

"If I move, it squeezes."

The floor shook beneath her as someone came into the trailer. The snake hissed. John's face turned white with a pale green over tint. Kenzie looked at him interestedly, wondering if he was going to faint or vomit first.

"What's going on in here?"

"Hang on a minute." Kenzie edged around the hole and went to the door. She herded the other firefighter ahead of her back out the door. "Hey, lieutenant, we've got a situation here." He came over, and she briefed him quickly. "And if anyone comes in, the snake gives John a squeeze." Not one of the brave male firefighters moved towards the trailer at the mention of snake, Kenzie noticed with a mental sneer.

"Can you kill it?"

"Not and not hurt JohnB as well. It's got its head right up next to his. I don't think I could hit it either with anything and not get him as well." That made all the other firefighters slink back a few more paces.

"Go keep him company. I'll call Animal Control." He said. Kenzie nodded and went back in.

"Help's on the way." She had told him. The snake was up near his mask. It was a beautiful animal in a slithery, spine-tingling way, with the head longer than Kenzie's hand. It was also very interested in JohnB's mask. Every time the tongue flickered in and out, another glisten of sweat beaded up on his forehead.

"I think my air pack is getting low," JohnB whispered. "If the alarm goes off..."

"Kenzie, Barstow, Animal Control will be here as soon as they can. They're on an emergency." The lieutenant called from outside.

"What the fuck do they think this is?" Kenzie muttered to herself, rewarded by JohnB's snort of laughter, then gasp as the snake squeezed. There was no way she was getting close to him to lift his mask. Not with that great head weaving around. She was not sure if the snake had teeth, but she would rather JohnB find out first.

"It's getting hard to breath, Kenzie."

"I got an idea." She fumbled for her radio. "Lieutenant, weren't there rabbit hutches out back? Grab me a couple, please. Bring them to the side door." She crept over to the door, and an anonymous hand shoved in two fuzzy bunnies. Kenzie crept back with them and placed them where the snake could see them. Its attention focused suddenly on the frightened bunnies now holding still in the knowledge that something was very wrong.

The snake began looping its way up JohnB until she could

barely see his head under the coils. The damn thing must be ten feet long. It rocketed off JohnB towards one of the bunnies, wrapping itself around the rabbit and vanishing in a writhing mass under the couch. Kenzie grabbed JohnB's harness as he sagged down. "Oh no, you don't, asshole. Stay on your feet. I'm not going down there with you. I hate spiders."

JohnB ripped off his helmet and mask, sucking in big breaths. The stink of flop sweat rose off him.

"You're not supposed to call senior firefighters assholes." He managed. Kenzie grinned at him.

"Screw with me again, buddy boy, and I'll stuff snakes into your turnouts. Let's get you out of there." Kenzie keyed her radio back on, and soon the tramp of heavy boots signaled help. Two of them held axes, just in case the evil snake mistook them for bunnies, Kenzie thought uncharitably.

JohnB's support was solid. She had even heard him defending her just before a union meeting.

"You just want to get into her pants." A male voice had smirked.

"Not my type, Sleazy. You know..." There was general laughter, and she imagined what his gestures had been—more curves than she possessed, undoubtedly.

They had gone out to a movie months later and, afterward, had been the most astonishing revelation of all. He had gone into her house with her, and Kenzie had expected him to make a move. Instead, he had cupped her chin in his hand.

"I like you just fine, Kenzie. But understand, you are not my type." He had looked deeply into her eyes. There was a message there, but she was not receiving it. Of course, she was not his type. He probably went for buxom blondes, not Shirley Temple clones. "Not my type." He repeated. Kenzie had frowned before understanding had dawned.

"Why you.... You put me through hell, and you're.... Jesus Christ, John. You bastard."

"I was doing what it was... suggested I do. Understand? It was not my idea. Look, we are both the odd men out. You even more than me." He had chuckled. "You watch my back, Fire Chick, and I'll watch yours. And the fire service can pray for mercy from Barstow and Stevenson." He added with a chuckle. From that night on, they had watched out for each other.

That is until tonight. Oh, god, thought Kenzie, what was she going to do without him. Never to climb into the jump seat beside him. Never to have their eyes meet and know precisely what the other was thinking. It was not fair. She should have died too. Memory forged back into her brain. Reminiscing had not made the pain lessen. She had just forgotten for a brief moment, protected by memory.

Tears leaked out from under her closed lids. The hot tears burned her face, where the mask had not protected her from the fire. Light from the doorway brightened her lids. Shoes clacked on the linoleum. Kenzie buried her head deeper into her pillow. Another nurse coming to give her sleeping pills or somehow disturb her.

The hands that touched her were hardly kind. Someone wrenched her up, and then the blows began, raining on her burns. Kenzie gasped in pain, too stunned to make a sound. "God damn you. All that for nothing." A sharp blow accompanied each whispered word. Kenzie could only cover her face with the arm that did not have an IV and to protect the burns. She had no idea who her attacker was. The IV ripped out, wrenching an incredible streak of agony up her arm. Kenzie pawed for the call button and pressed it desperately over and over again. The lights in the room blazed on, and immediately the blows stopped.

"Kenzie, Kenzie, stop. You'll hurt yourself. Nurse! Oh, thank heavens." Gone was the ring of anger in the voice, and instead worry flooded in. Kenzie's head whirled.

"What in the hell is going on in here?" One of the nurses crossed to the bed, coming between Kenzie and her attacker. "Call a code black." She yelled over her shoulder to a coworker. Kenzie looked up at her assailant through tears of pain.

Tina Sarkasian, her face contorted in concern. Tina's hand went to her mouth, and the other reached out to the nurse. So much compassion radiated off her that Kenzie suffered momentary disorientation. If not for the stinging agony in her face and her hand, she might well have believed the expression on Tina's face.

The nurse stood between Kenzie and Tina. Kenzie had the brief image of a German shepherd guarding her. The security guard and two other nurses came through the door. With an audience to play to, Tina calmed down, smoothing her hair and clothing.

"She attacked me." Kenzie choked out past a burning mouth and through adrenaline.

"Oh, Kenzie. I would never..." Her voice dripped with concern. "Nurse, I came in, and Kenzie was flailing around and crying. I was afraid she was going to hurt herself. Look, she's ripped out her IV."

"Like hell! She came in here and attacked me." Kenzie said as calmly as she could. Her face felt as if it was on fire, and she could taste blood. The first nurse pulled on rubber gloves and pulled some gauze pads out of a trauma tray. She gently pressed it onto Kenzie's hand and handed her another for her face. Kenzie patted at her face, eyeing the blood askance.

"Get her out of here." The other nurse snapped to the security guard, who moved towards Tina.

"I am going. I think Kenzie must be tripping on something. All these years we've been friends, and this is how you repay me?" Tina looked sorrowfully at Kenzie. The nurses looked doubtfully between Kenzie and Tina.

"Look, I'm not really sure what was going on, but Kenzie needs her rest." The first nurse said. "Under the circumstances, though, you should leave. It's past visiting hours."

"Of course. I'll be seeing you later, Kenzie." Tina smiled charmingly at each person in the hospital room, but her look at Kenzie made her shiver.

The security guard walked Tina out, and the other nurses left the room. The first nurse looked quizzically at Kenzie. She finished bandaging Kenzie's hand and started a new IV in the other.

"Friend of yours?"

"Oh, God, no."

"What happened?"

"I don't know. I was... just laying here, and she came in."

"Are you all right, ma'am?" The security guard came back in.

"No."

"That was Tina Sarkasian, the anchor from Channel 4 news." He informed them. Kenzie could see stars in his eyes. "She's promised to come back and do a story on hospital security." Kenzie rolled her eyes, and the nurse looked disgusted. "I can take down your side of the story if you want."

"Don't bother." Kenzie snapped.

"Okay." He went out, dreams of petty glory glowing in his eyes.

"Your face looks pretty bad." The nurse turned her face gently from side to side. "I'll make a note in the chart, and I'll be here all night, so don't worry about her coming back. Now, I'll get some silvadene cream, and let's see if we can't get the pain to lessen a bit. A sleeping pill might help, too."

Kenzie willingly accepted the cream, groaning slightly as the nurse smoothed the cream into the burns, but managed to palm the sleeping pill. There was no way she was going to be in a drugged sleep with Tina roaming the halls and the security guard half in lust with her. Sleep was long in coming, but she finally fell into exhaustion, JohnB's voice drifting through her dreams.

The next morning, Kenzie was ready to go as soon as the doctor had made rounds. Showering off the stink of fire and grief made her feel a little better, although she rediscovered that hot water on second-degree burns was a harrowing experience. The clean hospital gown felt good against her skin. She hoped Lee or someone would show up with some clothing; otherwise, she was tempted to walk out in her butt baring hospital gown. JohnB would laugh...

Grief caught her unaware, and she collapsed onto the bed, curled around her pain and anguish, sobbing into her hands so that the nurses would not hear. Gentle hands smoothed back her hair, and Kenzie rolled to her feet, smacking the hands away. Lee faced her across the bed. Kenzie sat back down, heart pounding and breathless. The too ready tears sprang into her eyes.

"Good grief. Are you alright, Kenz?" At her mute headshake,

he went around the bed and gently folded her into his arms. After she had calmed a little, he looked at her more closely. "You got beat up a whole lot worse than it seemed yesterday."

"I got beat up last night. Your girlfriend paid me a visit." Kenzie peered into the tiny mirror attached to the bed tray. There was a long, red-skinned mark probably from a fingernail or a ring. One eye was blackening, and her lip was swollen and bleeding. She touched the fat lip with a wince and licked it.

"Girlfriend? You mean... Tina?"

"In the flesh. She paid me a little visit that started in screaming and slapping. And ending in having the nurses assume I was crazed with grief." Kenzie's words held a wealth of bitterness.

"That's... interesting." Lee frowned.

"Is Flower okay?"

"He missed you. I fed him, but I'm not sure he ate anything."

"Thank you." She looked away, mustering self-control. "Did you bring my clothes?" Kenzie asked, hopefully. Lee held out a shopping bag. Kenzie took it and headed for the bathroom. Lee had thought to bring her softest clothes: sweats and a loose t-shirt, one without a firefighter symbol or logo on it, Kenzie noticed gratefully. He must have had to dig through a lot of clothes to find one, she thought with a shaky laugh.

"So, what did Tina say?" Lee asked as Kenzie came back out.

"I don't remember. All I remember is Tina hitting me."

"Hmm. Ready to go?"

"Oh, yes. I'm discharged. Let's blow this joint before the nurses bring a wheelchair." Kenzie gathered up a garbage bag that stank of the house fire. She swayed slightly, the odor directly connecting into her memories, and for a moment, Lee thought she was going to go down. He reached out for the bag.

Kenzie snatched it back.

"I can carry my own gear." She marched out of the room, Lee following silently. This was going to be a dilly of a day. Kenzie waved off the wheelchair-wielding nurse. Lee met the nurse's eyes with a headshake. This was not the time to challenge Kenzie. As they left the hospital, only Gordo was waiting outside. He snapped a few pictures and left before Lee could intercept him.

"What a creep," Lee muttered. "Home, Kenz?"

"No. First to John's mom's house." Kenzie gave him directions during an otherwise silent drive. He could feel the tension radiating off her, increasing as they neared the low-slung ranch style.

Once the car stopped, Kenzie sat very still for a few moments, then threw herself out of the car, stalking up to the house as if she did not go right then and there, she would lose her nerve. Lee followed her, waiting patiently as Kenzie gave herself a mental shake before knocking on the door. One of John's sisters, face blotched from crying, opened the door.

"I just... wanted to say... I'm sorry." Kenzie squeezed out before bursting into tears. For a moment, she stood alone, shoulders hunched and tears streaming down her face before John's mother came out and enveloped Kenzie in a hug.

"Oh, Kenzie, thank you for coming." JohnB's mother was in a state of calm grief, holding up for all the people who now depended on her to bear their grief for her son's passing. Kenzie struggled with her grief, unwilling to add more to this woman who had been so kind to her over the years that Kenzie had been John's friend. Once in the house, Lee stood to one side, watching as John's best friend grieved with his family. One of the sisters stood apart from the group, eyes dry. Lee kept an eye on her, expecting an outburst. As soon as Kenzie had sat down, she pounced.

"Johnny always said women shouldn't be firefighters." Her voice was cold and harsh. Kenzie flinched as if she had been physically hit. Lee crept in between the two women. He knew that this scene had to play out for John's sister's sake, but he had no desire to see this woman destroy Kenzie.

"Now, Leeann..." John's mother started.

"If another man had been in the fire with Johnny, he wouldn't have died." The sister continued over her mother's words.

"It was a trap," Kenzie answered steadily, her tears dried up. "It wouldn't have mattered if a dozen men had been on the line. The whole house was a trap. We came very close to losing a lot more firefighters."

"Then why weren't you in front?"

"Because... John... liked to be first in. He always wanted to be the first to go into the belly of the beast. It was what John lived for." Kenzie was calm and under complete control. Lee watched her warily. She was too calm, too collected. "I would never have done anything to hurt him. He was my best friend, and I will miss him every day for the rest of my life."

The silence that followed was almost a prayer, and Kenzie's words seemed to satisfy some of the family. John's mother asked her to say a few words at the funeral, and Kenzie agreed, hugging the woman one more time.

"Home?" Lee asked once they were back in his truck.

"To the house." Kenzie fastened her seat belt and then stared straight ahead.

"I don't think that's a good idea."

"I didn't ask you if you thought it was a good idea. I said I want to go to the house. You can take me there, or I'll walk."

She grabbed the door handle. The strain under her voice made her words crack like a whip. Lee reined in his temper.

"The investigators will be at work. It's a crime scene, Kenz."

"No, shit. I want to go to the house." She repeated. Lee looked at her profile, sighed, and started the engine. She was perfectly capable of getting out and walking there. Her face was set in stone.

Once in front of the house, Kenzie refused to look at it. Lee glanced around, the entire scene playing in his head. A small shrine of flowers made a bright spot on the otherwise bleak scene. Fires scenes were soggy places, and mud puddles glistened, marking where the fire engine had stood and the path the hoses had taken.

Crime scene tape secured the building, and several vehicles were clustered in the driveway. Bob Chu pulled himself away from a knot of men and walked over. Lee lowered Kenzie's window. She did not move. She could not move. Even to look at the place was awful. Her fingers were clenched so tightly on the door handle that Lee was surprised not to hear the plastic give way.

"Can I help... Aw, Kenzie." Bob's voice went from official to soft as he bent down to the window. He reached out and touched her shoulder, patting awkwardly. Kenzie kept her face resolutely forward, a muscle jumping in her jaw.

"It was a trap, Kenzie. The first person across the floor didn't stand a chance." A single choked groan escaped her. "Go home and rest. We need you back on the fire line. We have to catch this asshole." Bob looked curiously at Lee, then nodded in respect and straightened, tapping the top of the truck. Lee pulled away from the house and headed back towards Kenzie's townhouse.

Flower was hysterically glad to see Kenzie. They had been

together twenty-four /seven for years, and Flower had not liked being abandoned. Kenzie hugged the dog until he calmed down and then held him tightly, drawing strength from him. When he struggled to get loose, she let him and then started to wander aimlessly around the house. Lee watched silently. He had seen this look before, in people stretched too tightly, just before some spectacular show of self-destruction, and he knew better than to leave her alone or trust her to one of her girlfriends who might not know what to do. She picked up the fire scene candle and stood for a moment, shifting from foot to foot.

"It wasn't your fault, Kenz."

"No. It's yours, dammit. Why couldn't you tell me the truth? I might have had a chance to catch the arsonist." Muscle made hard from years of working out and hauling hoses bunched. She threw the candle against the wall furthest from Lee. It dented the sheetrock, splattered into a greasy mess, and slid to the floor. Lee tensed, even though the candle had not been meant for him.

"That's not fair, Kenzie."

"Fair? Fair? Don't give me fair, bud. It's not fair that John is dead." Kenzie's grip on her temper and grief slipped. She snatched one candle after another off the shelf and threw them. She screamed and raged, all the hurt coming out. Flower slunk off to hide in the bedroom. Lee did his best not to listen to her words, but some of them hit home in an excruciatingly painful manner.

"Why in the hell are you here anyway?" She stopped raging and stood in front of Lee. Her face was flushed, sweaty and her hands clenched. Lee eased to his feet in case she decided to make the attack physical.

"Because..." Lee grimaced. "Because I heard you scream."

"I never screamed. It's damned hard to scream in a face mask." Kenzie snapped.

Lee looked at her calmly. He had been watching the crowd at the fire, looking for someone who was acting wrong. Arsonists almost always returned to the scene of their crime. He had turned back to see Kenzie and JohnB going into the house. Her name was emblazoned on the back of her turnouts, but he would recognize her anywhere, even covered with 50 pounds of Nomex and gear. They went into the house. Seconds passed. The firefighters who had gone in the side door had rocketed out, calling for foam, whatever that meant.

Over the din of the fire ground, he had heard Kenzie scream. He was halfway across the lawn before the heat of the fire stopped him. No one else reacted, more focused on whatever the other firefighters were wanting. Lee had cursed himself for a fool, slinking back to his patrol car. Shrill bleating cut across the commotion and noise, the insistent scream of a PSD. The fire ground exploded into high gear, firefighters racing into the house carrying extinguishers, laying more lines.

Minutes later, a lifetime later, two firefighters burst out of the house, dragging a body with them. They pulled off her hood, and the bright gold curls caught the firelight. Kenzie started to fight them. He had gone to her, drawn by something more potent than heart deep betrayal. He was definitely a fool. All that long day, he had sat with her until the very end, unable to leave her. Since Lee had not wanted to deal with Kenzie, he had never bothered to return her house key, he was able to take Flower home and feed him. Flower was taken home and fed. Lee had found her parents' number and had his mother call them. He had followed that up with a harrowing day chauffeuring her around. And why? Because of a scream. And because he was a fool.

"I heard you scream. And when the medics dragged you out... " Lee shrugged. "You are one bad patient. I thought the medics could use some help." Kenzie snorted in amusement, then choked on a sob. The rage refocused itself as grief, and Lee wrapped his arms around her, letting her cry in private. He could hear the sirens in the distance, closing rapidly. Lee rolled his eyes. The joy of living in a row of townhouses.

Two patrol officers came cautiously into Kenzie's house, eyebrows going up as they saw him there.

"What's up, Lee?" Asked one, and the other gently separated Kenzie from him, taking stock of the bruises on her face.

"The firefighter who died last night. She was his partner. She was in the fire with him last night." Lee said softly. "She's gotten to the anger stage of grief."

"It's not Lee's fault. He's only been helping me. I'm the one doing all the screaming." Kenzie spoke up, her voice hoarse.

The two men conferred for a moment, taking stock of the broken candles and the dog peering down the stairs.

"You be careful, Lee. Another call from this address and we'll have to do something. You take care, then. And..." One of them reached out to touch her arm. "I'm sorry for your loss." Kenzie wrapped her arms around herself, nodding thanks but not trusting to speak.

They went out, closing the door behind them. Lee led her to the couch and sat her down, putting his arm around her. Flower came out of hiding to rest his head on Kenzie's leg and stare up at her.

"What something to eat or drink?"

"No, thanks." Silence reigned for a time. Flower pricked

up his ears, looking towards the door as it opened slowly. Lee turned to see an older man and woman pushing through the door and into the room.

"Oh, my poor baby." The woman said, hurrying across the room and gathering Kenzie away from Lee. Kenzie clung to her.

"Mom. Dad." Kenzie managed. Lee reached out and smoothed down her hair. When he looked up, Kenzie's father watched him with the penetrating look fathers reserve for dubious dates. The older man had her bright green eyes, Lee noticed irreverently, but the curls must come from some other relative. The iron-grey hair was short and straight.

"I assume you're Lee. Bill Stevenson. Kenzie's dad." He added just in case Lee was unaware of his identity. He held out a large, calloused hand. Lee took it after a moment's hesitation.

"Sir." Nothing else came to mind. The two men warily examined each other.

"Thanks for having your mother call us." Bill Stevenson finally said. Lee nodded once and dropped his eyes. Quietly, he left the house, closing the door behind him. He was drained. It had been an exhausting twenty-four hours.

By the day of JohnB's funeral, Kenzie had mastered her grief. It had been a point of pride that she never cried in front of her brother firefighters, and she had no intention of starting now. Every firefighter on her shift, including the powers that be, would be watching her like a cat watching a wounded bird.

Her career depended on not making a mistake or being seen as too feminine. It sometimes seemed so pointless. Why showing emotion was taboo but telling macho jokes about death and gore was acceptable. Testosterone was one hormone

Kenzie had no desire to have a closer acquaintance with. It made men remarkably irrational. She had chosen to be a lone female in an all-male field, and this was the price she had to pay.

At first light on the morning of the funeral, Kenzie was at the station, polishing the engine that would be used to carry JohnB's coffin. She was joined by the silent group of firefighters who would attend the funeral, riding in the engine as an honor guard, and those who would be staying behind at the station to protect and serve. Like every other firefighter funeral, the funeral would be one of pomp, tradition, and intense media coverage. Especially after 9/11, firefighter funerals had become popular media fare. It was a point of pride that the engine would be spotless, even the interiors of the equipment boxes which no one would ever see. They worked silently.

Already, fire engines were lining the street in front of Station One. The firefighters riding in them were mostly silent, waiting. Occasional subdued laughter or groans at the end of the war stories the different departments were undoubtedly sharing drifted over to the firehouse. Fire departments from all over the US had sent representatives, and practically every department in the state had sent an engine to be part of the procession.

The funeral procession would pass by every fire department in the city either on its way to the memorial service or on the way to the cemetery. That way, every firefighter, on or off duty, could pay his respects. People would line the streets, watching in honor, in avid curiosity, in excitement. Somewhere in the crowd, Kenzie knew the arsonist would be watching. Hatred shook her frame. She would make no promises aloud, but she would find the arsonist and somehow exact her revenge.

Chris Malone, the paramedic, came out into the bay, and

Kenzie focused every iota of her being on polishing a tiny corner of the engine. She had yet to forgive him for his automatic assumption that she had somehow screwed up on the day of the JohnB's death.

"Hey, Kenz." Malone's voice was deeper than normal in embarrassment.

"Yeah?" Kenzie did not stop her work.

"I'm sorry... I spoke without thinking, when, when I asked, you know..." The words were hard for him, choking him, Kenzie thought viciously. Maybe one of the words would do the trick, and he would choke permanently. "It wasn't your fault. It was..."

Kenzie turned around, anger rising up in a red tide. His face became a pinprick in a sea of rage. She wanted nothing more than to scream at him or swear or throw the can of polish or somehow react, but to do so would be a fatal mistake. All her hard-earned respect would evaporate in a flurry of jokes about menstruation and female hormones.

"I accept your apology. Leave it at that." Kenzie refused to smile, to weaken her position in his eyes. She bit the insides of her mouth to steady her lips, shaking either in anger or in grief, it did not matter. Malone stood for another embarrassed moment.

"What else needs to be done?" He asked. The other firefighters who had stopped work to watch the exchange all exchanged significant looks and went back to work. Kenzie worked with her head down until the rage and grief had subsided. She could not care less about what he did next, as long as he was not near her.

Kenzie watched the long black hearse pull into the station driveway. One of the firefighters waved him to park in front of the waiting engine. Under her shirt, she could feel her stomach muscles trembling. Six firefighters removed the coffin from the hearse and carried it into the station bay. Someone pressed the button to lower the bay door, leaving them in privacy. The funeral director lurked in the background, looking professionally solemn. She wished he would go away. It felt as though he were feeding off their grief.

JohnB's brother firefighters gathered around his coffin in the privacy of their bay. It was closed, and Kenzie knew everyone was trying not to picture what was under the lid. Those who knew looked sick. Rookie firefighters were shown films of burn victims, and most paramedics had spent time in burn wards while they were training. Death by fire was a gruesome way to go.

The city chaplain hurried in to lead a prayer and say a few words of comfort. Just before John's coffin was loaded onto the hose bed, Kenzie pressed her fingers to the top, silently vowing revenge. They left smudges on the black wood, and she obsessively rubbed them off with the cuff of her shirt.

Kenzie climbed into her seat in the back of the engine cab. Kurt sat next to her. In JohnB's place. For a moment, Kenzie hated her friend. The engine rumbled to life, and they pulled out of the bay. As they passed the long line of fire engines, ladder trucks, and ambulances, each started their engines. An errant thought about global warming flitted through Kenzie's brain, and she ruthlessly suppressed it. This was no time for stupid, irreverent thoughts.

Their engine finally came to the head of the procession, just in front of the black limousine carrying John's family. As expected, people lined the route. Kenzie leaned her head on the window glass, watching their faces flow by. In front of each station, the on-duty firefighters stood quietly at attention as their fallen brother passed by. There were tears on most faces. It seemed profoundly unfair that they could cry, and she could not.

The media was out in full force. The Channel 4 cameras were at the top of the church steps. Kenzie could imagine Tina's face on the evening news, reflecting professional sorrow as she reported on the day's events. She gritted her teeth. Gordo roved the crowd, getting his human-interest shots.

Kenzie had seen his now-famous photo. He had had the gall to mail several copies to her, even as it had hit the wires and been published in every newspaper with AP access. It had gone viral as well, speeding around the world.She had ripped her first copy to shreds and then reconsidered, tucking another copy into a book she never read. Maybe someday, she would be able to look at it without her heart being torn from her chest.

They escorted the coffin to the front of the church and took their seats. Row after row of white-shirted officers and grey shirted line firefighters filled the pews behind them. The church was packed, but the crowd was silent. It was somehow wrong for it to be so quiet. Kenzie sat between Kurt and their lieutenant.

The preacher began the service, reading scripture, praising John. Kenzie tried not to listen too closely. The preacher's words would shatter her defenses. John would never forgive her if she broke down in the middle of his funeral. Kenzie snickered softly, earning a frown from the Lieutenant, who apparently was not sure if she was losing her mind or her manners. Then it was her turn.

Kenzie's shoes sounded too loud as she made her way to the podium. Seated behind the serving firefighters, her father nodded to her, his full dress uniform glittery with gold trim. Her mother pressed her fingers to her lips in a wish for good luck. Further back, a pew of blue and white and brown and tan caught her eyes. Lee. And his fellow law enforcement officers. For a long moment, Kenzie gazed at Lee, feeling strength flow into her and a calmness that chased away the sorrow.

"When John and I officially met, on my first day of rookie school, we hated each other. I could think of one word that described him perfectly, and that was T-O-O, too. He was too big, too loud, too aggressive, too much to deal with. It took a long time for me to understand that under all that attitude was a great man.

"I remember his rage at the injustices we face every day, the injustice of children dying, or the injustice that comes at the wheel of drunk drivers, or at the rampant stupidity that risks our lives, the lives of the firefighters he served with. John's heart was big, and he cared. Most of all, he loved his brother firefighters, and nothing was too good for us. John's laugh was legendary, and he could be heard over the sound of the siren and engine. However, he did not laugh only at others.

"John laughed regardless of who was the butt of a joke, and he could take jokes as well as he dished out. On... his last day, we rigged up a dead snake to scare anyone opening the bay door. John screamed louder and laughed longer when it was his turn to open the door. And those of you who knew him well know how much John hated snakes.

"John's abilities as a firefighter were never hampered by his size. Sometimes, I swear he was made of rubber and could fit through spaces I didn't think a cat could crawl through. His strength was amazing, and he handled the jaws as if they weighed nothing. His speed was unequaled in our department, and he made rescues almost easy." Kenzie stopped and rubbed her forehead, marshaling her self-control. She could hear John laughing.

"I came to love John as my best friend, my partner, and a damned fine firefighter. If there is a heaven, John is there now, playing tricks on the angels and making plans to storm hell and put out all the fires. When John's life was stolen from him, everyone lost. His parents. His sisters. His brother firefighters. His friends. The people we serve and protect. We lost a hero in every sense of the word." Kenzie wanted to add more, but her voice was starting to tremble, and she knew she had done her best. Any more would push the limits of her control. She looked around the room once more, meeting eyes, and then walked back to her seat. The Lieutenant reached out and took her hand, squeezing it gently before letting go.

The fire chaplain took his place at the front of the chapel and motioned his hand to the traditional table set for a firefighter service.

"To my right is a table set for one. This table is set for John Barstow, who is missing from our midst today. To the community, he was a firefighter. To us, he was our brother. He is unable to be with us today. Please allow me to share the symbolism of this table that has been set for this fallen firefighter. The white tablecloth symbolizes the purity of his intentions to respond to his department's every call. The floral arrangement also tells a story. The red rose is for those who made the ultimate sacrifice – John gave his life so that others could live. The white rose is for those who witnessed and experienced tragedy and destruction firsthand and are still with us today." His eyes swept across the firefighters. "A slice of lemon is on the plate to remind us of his bitter fate. There is salt on the plate, symbolic of the tears shed by friends and family. The glass is inverted – – he cannot toast with us. The chair is empty – – he is not here, but we will never forget him." Kenzie crushed her hands together, trying not to hear his words.

Once the funeral was over, the fire trucks headed to the cemetery for the last of the funeral. Kenzie could only feel dull and tired. She was not looking forward to the Last Call. As they entered the cemetery and crawled to the grave, the pipers began to skirl *Amazing Grace*. If she had not disliked the song before, Kenzie believed that she would never be able to hear it again without feeling grief and revulsion.

They gathered at the graveside and waited in silence. One of the radios crackled to life.

"Firefighter John Barstow– Control. Firefighter John Barstow – Control" There was a long silence. "Having heard no response from Firefighter John Barstow, we know that John Barstow has responded to his last call on earth and that the fire department in the hereafter has a new responder. Firefighter John Barstow completed his tour as a Firefighter in this life. Be safe until we meet again. Control clear at 15:20 hours." Kenzie turned and quietly made her way back to the engine where she could cry in privacy.

The funeral was creating an odd sensation in his head. The grief fed his need for drama. He could almost feel energy draining off the mourners and into him. He had felt sorrow and guilt when he had heard about John and then thought about Kenzie. It had made him swear to never set another fire. The snake could go whisper in someone else's ear. He felt a little odd without the sibilant voice of the snake whispering in his ear and the voice of fire speaking to his soul. The silence made him feel strong.

Chapter 14

The funeral was over. Kenzie's parents had gone home. The phone was silent. Her friends were back in the groove of their own lives, forgetting that Kenzie had not yet returned to hers. After his brief appearance during the fire and the day after, Lee had vanished back into his own existence. She had not really expected him to stick around, but she missed him even more for the brief contact.

Kenzie was very bored. Light duty at the fire station was just that, the tedium of writing reports, running errands, cooking, and other tasks that did not come close to the fun and challenge of firefighting and rescues. As soon as the burns had healed, she could return to full duty, and that would be any day now.

The chaplain and the city-selected mental health counselor tried to talk to her to get some idea of her emotional status. Kenzie was having none of that. Like most of her fellow firefighters, she assumed that nothing, not medical reports, financial problems, or most especially mental health concerns, were really confidential, and admitting weakness or fear would only earn her trouble.

She went on achingly empty of any feeling except the burning desire to catch the arsonist and the fear of ever going into another burning building. She woke up regularly at night, drenched in sweat, heart pounding, holding onto the bed as the floor in her dreams spun away from her feet. She was so exhausted.

Perhaps the worst of it was work. Since Kenzie was on light duty, she kept regular hours of seven a.m. to four p.m., and she saw all the firefighters at her station. Most of her co-workers, at some point, would herd her away from the activity of the fire station with their main goal of talking about JohnB and their own fears as they touched on the fire service.

She realized she had been raised to the status of some sort of vestal virgin— to tell fears to in hopes that she would intervene with the gods of fire. She had survived trial by fire, and in her co-workers' unexamined inner superstitions, she was either very good luck or very bad luck. At any rate, she listened and was ripped apart anew each day. The few that did not come to talk seemed to hold her responsible for JohnB's death. It was easier to hide out in her room than to deal with the ones who needed to talk and those who watched her with suspicion.

She had a new helmet as well. Hers had been melted into a blob of seared yellow plastic. This new one was shiny and clean, and only rookies wore clean turnouts. A few fires would make a difference, at least to the shininess. Kenzie sighed as she hung it up. Her nickname had not been put on this one, and she was not sure she would change the helmet's barrenness. It seemed to match her mood.

Kenzie went to her final doctor visit, where the doctor declared that the burns were healed enough to go back to full duty status, and she found herself once again in the jump seat of the engine. The next few shifts were quiet enough, mostly medical calls, but each tone out of the station crews left her limp with dread. She carried on, aware that everyone from the lowest rookie to the chief was watching her.

A man might just possibly be able to get by after having a breakdown, whether of nerve or emotion, but if she so much as twitched, her career would be over. She lay awake for hours each night, unable to sleep because of the heart-pounding dreams that made each night a particular terror. Kenzie pondered her career choices during those long hours and decided that there was not much else other than firefighting she would rather do. She would just have to suck it up and go on one step at a time, just like rookie school. Except with no friend at the end to make the trip worthwhile.

He paced around his house, arguing with the voice in his head. The snake had become invisible and somehow entwined with the voice of the Fire, whispering in his ear. This voice told him that he would be invincible if he caused another death, like the evil sorcerers of legend. He exulted in his heart, careful to keep a professionally somber face to the public. The part of him that knew he had to stop was unhappy, and so was the part that listened to the snake. He wanted to light a match. He craved the flame at the end of the match. The desire to burn was eating away at his resolve to quit. He could almost feel the heat of fire on his fingers, his face.

The perfect fire came to him as he watched videos of the other fires. Revenge against the snake, against Kenzie, and maybe even a little more death. Death had made regular arson fires seem tame, and he wanted, needed, craved the extra excitement of causing a death through his beloved fires. So, he had begun planning until all the factors came together. The Perfect Storm, ha, they would be making movies about this fire for years to come.

Daily fire station life went on. Kenzie and Kurt were on kitchen duty. At least she did not have fridge duty this time, Kenzie thought. Not that the fridge ever reached the scary condition her personal at-home fridge had on a few occasions when the deli turkey opened the door and walked out. However, with Kurt on fridge duty, she may as well be cleaning it out herself, she thought ruefully as he brought yet another container to her.

"It's just a bit of mold. Shouldn't hurt anyone." He said, with big starving puppy dog eyes. Kurt could not bear to throw out food of any description, even when it oozed out of its container and showed signs of evolving intelligence.

"It's nasty." Kenzie shrugged. "Would your dog eat it?" Kenzie thought about Kurt's overly finicky mutt. The joke was Kurt ate the scraps the dog left behind.

"Probably not." Kurt looked ruefully at the leftovers.

"Into the garbage, then." Kenzie retreated to the other side of the kitchen, where she sorted through notices on the bulletin board. Someone had a couch for sale. Two weeks old. A job opening. Past the due date. She wadded it up, tossing it into the garbage can. Another one, the city was replacing sewer pipes in the Mesa Heights neighborhood. The pipes had been failing at alarming rates.

Along with that, they would be checking the water main, installed at the same time by the same contractor. Kenzie checked the date. They would be just beginning the project today. That meant the water would be off on a rolling basis. Good thing that this area of town housed the wealthier families, and the homes were better constructed.

"Station One, dispatch. Toning out on shed fire, 1501 Mason. Station one, toning out on shed fire. 1501 Mason." Kenzie threw the outdated notices into the trash, shut Flower into his kennel, and walked quickly to the fire engine. Shed fire. Probably not too bad. No going into the belly of the beast today.

The crowd of neighbors, children, and excitement marked the fire's location with pinpoint accuracy. Several people waved them in. Kenzie hopped out of the engine and pulled the attack hose off the bed. With Kurt, she trotted back to the rear of the house. On the way, they passed a tiny, shivering dog, its fur in wet mats and misery written all over its face. Kenzie gave it a curious look. At least it did not seem particularly interested in attacking them. Small dogs were infinitely worse than big ones when it came to overreacting on emergency scenes. Neighbors had garden hoses dragged over and were spraying water on a wooden doghouse.

"I guess that's our shed."

"Looks mostly out to me." Kurt turned the nozzle on and sprayed water on the smoldering remains. Once it was out, Kenzie dropped to her knees to peer inside. The stink of wet burned straw drifted out to her, and she stirred the mess a little so that the water could soak more thoroughly.

"I just didn't want that little mutt sleeping inside anymore. Dogs belong outside. Not on my bed." The dog's owner was explaining to the lieutenant.

"What did you do to the doghouse?"

"I filled it with straw and hung a work light inside it to keep Precious warm." The man replied. Someone had had the presence of mind to unplug the light when the fire started, Kenzie realized. Otherwise, it could have been a much more interesting fire. Water, fire, and electricity made for hellacious scenes. She looked more closely at the doghouse and then stood blinking for a few seconds while her brain processed the scene.

A bag of fertilizer held down one side of the makeshift roof; a gallon of chain saw oil secured the other.

"Saints preserve us from fools," Kenzie muttered her father's favorite prayer.

"What?" Kurt said.

"The mutt's owner just built himself a bomb," Kenzie said, gesturing to the doghouse. Kurt's eyebrows climbed under his helmet.

"Oh, good Christ," Kurt exclaimed. "Hey, Lieutenant. Take a look at this."

"What? What?" The doghouse owner hurried over behind the lieutenant.

"Norman. Norman. What in the hell is going on here?" A piercing voice scattered the onlookers. A large woman in a brightly flowered muumuu was bearing down on them. Kenzie could just barely see Precious tucked under one massive arm.

"We...uh... there was a fire in the doghouse." The man managed. Kurt and Kenzie began edging away. The lieutenant looked on with an expression that Kenzie recognized as a finely tuned appreciation of irony.

"I said Precious isn't sleeping out here." The woman growled.

"Well, not now." The man replied glumly.

"And you." The woman turned on the lieutenant next, jabbing a large finger in his direction. From the safety of her arm, the little dog growled, showing perfect little teeth. "You parked that fire truck on my grass AND blocked the driveway. You get it moved before it ruins my grass." Snickers ran through the watching firefighters. The lieutenant's face grew very set.

"Yes, ma'am. As soon as I get this report finished."

"I mean now." The woman barked.

"Yes, ma'am." He glanced up at the observing firefighters, all valiantly suppressing smirks, and gestured to the hose. Quickly, they hurried to clean up. "Now, sir, do you realize what fertilizer and chain saw oil make if they mix, especially with a heat source?" The man slowly shook his head in response. "A massive explosion."

"A what?"

"You turned...er... Presh... your dog's house into a bomb. If your neighbors had not been quick with the garden hose, we'd have had a pretty impressive explosion."

"Norman." The rising inflection of the woman's voice moved the neighbors further away. As she began to berate the man, the lieutenant came up to the other firefighters.

"Come on. Let's get the hell out of here before she starts on us."

"I'm glad I'm not a cop," Kurt said as the police moved in on an incipient domestic.

Looking behind them, Kenzie could see that the engine's rear tires had left ruts in the lawn where the soil had been softened by perpetually leaking water pump. Kenzie cringed. At least she would not have to deal with the phone call the station would be getting as soon as Mrs. Norman had finished browbeating Norman. Snickers washed through the fire engine, followed by almost hysterical laughter. Each time the laughter died away; someone would set it off again. Kenzie felt a huge relief fill her. This was a healing time.

The laughter made a difference. For the first time since JohnB's death, Kenzie enjoyed work and training Flower and spent an ordinary evening at the station. The insurance company had given her sick time, but soon the calls for Flower's services would start again. The arsonist would strike again. The desire to set fires was too strong now for the arsonist to stop. The only way to stop him would be to catch him, and she would somehow, someway catch the bastard. This she promised solemnly to herself and to JohnB's memory.

Chapter 15

Kenzie's first house fire since John's death came the next duty day, very early before the shift changed over.

"Station one, dispatch. Toning out house fire. 1250 Mesa Terrace. House fire 1250 Mesa Terrace. Time is 0600." A few grumbles met the dispatch. Since it was still Kenzie's shift, her crew would go, even thirty minutes before crew change. The earliest arriving firefighters saw them off and then went to start their morning chores.

"Okay, guys. We have no water. City's replacing the main up there. The good news is most of the residents are probably gone. Make every gallon count." The lieutenant briefed them quickly over the headphones. Kenzie and Kurt exchanged grimaces. Every firefighter knew how to put out fires with the minimum of water— the Navy's spray and smother technique for shipboard fire suppression. A good firefighter could put out a lot of fire with 1,000 gallons of water carried in the engine's tank.

The foreman of the water replacement crew met them in front of the burning house.

"We can't get the water on for another two, maybe three hours. If we turn the main on now, it'll look like Old Faithful out here. We are turned off for six blocks around. I've called in extra crews, but we can only go so fast." He reported.

"Okay." The lieutenant turned from the foreman to his waiting firefighters. "Do your best with the tank. Kurt, Little Bob, you're first in, clear the house. I'll call for reserves." As the assigned firefighters trotted off, Kenzie waited for her orders. The lieutenant picked up his radio. "Dispatch, engine one. Roll the tanker from Station One."

He was calling up her station's reserve tanker with an extra 1,000 gallons of water and two additional firefighters, just in case. Kenzie glanced over at the apparatus operator standing by the pump panel. He was calmly watching the dials on the panel to make sure that water would flow steadily. The smoke roiling out of the house was turning white, a sure sign the fire was coming under control.

He watched the activity from behind a curtain. His latest stroke of genius had been to experiment with timing devices. So far, they had worked brilliantly. But then, how could he fail? He was the god of fire. Every other fire had been a success. He could not fail. The firefighters scurried around like the insignificant roaches they were. He recognized Kenzie by the name at the bottom of her bunker coat. It was pure genius, this setup. He would wait until they almost had the fire out. And then he would create fire. The firefighters were cautious now, not going into the house. They did not want to lose another man, but they would. He would see to that. He would have to consider the next death carefully. Careful planning would be required to feed his beloved Fire. And now to be the god. Now to assume his rightful place, just as the snake. He pressed the trigger on the radio control box.

Kenzie helped Kurt change out his air pack when the windows in the house across the street exploded outward in a spectacular sparkle of glass shards and window framing. Flame leaped up and out the windows, reaching high up along the house. The air rushing away from the explosion knocked her into Kurt, flipping her over his back. She landed on the grass with a grunt and the knowledge that there would be many bruises.

For a brief second, a curtain flapped in the wind created by the fire. It burst into flame and vanished a millisecond later—an accelerated fire. The arsonist had stuck again. As they picked themselves up, Kurt swore softly. What was left of 1,000 gallons was not going to touch this one. Not even the pumper was going to help.

"Alrighty then," Lieutenant muttered before picking up his radio. "Dispatch, engine one. Roll engine two. Roll medic two. Alert station five. Notify the Chief that we have a three-alarm fire."

"Engine one, dispatch. Roll engine two. Roll medic two. Station two, dispatch..." Dispatch's voice faded as the lieutenant looked around the fire ground. He turned to Kenzie, determination on his face. "Kenzie, go find us a swimming pool. Someone in this neighborhood has to have one."

Kenzie raised a hand and jogged off to peer over fences. Four houses down, she found a pool, and for once, there was no crazed, vicious dog to be controlled. She jogged back to report.

"Pumper one, engine one. Pull up to 1257 Mesa Terrace. Draft off the swimming pool." "The lieutenant's voice remained calm, but Kenzie could hear a thread of strain. Activity kicked into a new high as police began evacuating the surrounding houses. As they had expected, most of the residents had left rather than put up with no water. Mostly what was left were maids and gardeners, and they gathered in a chattering bunch beyond the police line. A media truck roared up, disgorging a cameraman and a reporter.

"Kenzie, get that fence down." The lieutenant snapped. Kenzie trotted back to the future drafting pool with an axe and a pair of bolt cutters. The gate was locked, but a wooden fence was not exactly an impediment. She removed a panel of the fence and cut the chain-link fence around the pool.

The wailing of the pumper truck's siren preceded its arrival on the hilltop. Kenzie waved them over, guiding the pumper truck into place. The van carrying extra equipment and the B shift firefighters the lieutenant had called on scene screamed up just behind the pumper, and they raced past, pulling all the way to Engine One to get their orders. Several jogged back to lay the suction line from the pumper to the swimming pool. These were long hard sections of hose that would be attached to the pumper's 5-inch suction port. The pumper could then pull water, or draft, from the pool, feed it through the pump to the fire hoses to the engine where it would go to feed the hand lines.

Already firefighters were snaking hoses between the vehicles, and the pumper's AO stood ready to charge the lines into the fire engine. Kenzie fished a few pool toys and the automatic vacuum out of the pool. They would jam and damage the pumper if they were sucked into the hard lines.

"Draft ready." One of the B shift firefighters called out.

"Drafting," The pumper engineer called back. The hard-line vibrated for a moment as it filled with water. "Ready pumper." He called to the engineer on the engine. The soft lines between the pumper and the engine gently vibrated and then grew hard as water rushed toward the engine. Firefighters pulled hoses towards the second house. At the first house, they were just starting to overhaul.

Kenzie jogged back to her engine for more orders. Engine two and the chief arrived simultaneously, and Kenzie could see the relief in the Lieutenant's face as he handed off the fire scene to a firefighter who had been putting fires out while most of his crew was playing with Tonka fire engines in the sandbox.

Oh, God, this was fun. Four fire engines. Two ambulances. Six police cars. Two full shifts of firefighters. Soon he would have all the shifts. He sniggered. Maybe he would torch one of the high-rise dorms next—multiple fires on multiple floors. Someone pounded on the door, and he waited silently, hidden from view. He heard the police clear the house and move on. The fire was ready to go in this house. He had used gasoline to make the fire extra hot and to ensure maximum confusion and smoke so he could escape out the back door. He could smell the fumes. Revenge was his. Fire was his. This house would be a pleasure to burn. He hated the thick carpeting. The fancy draperies. The expensive and happily flammable furnishings. Most of all, he hated the occupant. He turned, his feet scuffing through the thick carpet. Kneeling, he reached for the detonator. Static electricity leaped from his finger into the fumes from the gasoline.

Kenzie stood next to the chief as he handed out orders. The incident command structure had just increased, and she became the liaison, pulled off the fire line, partly to her relief, partly to her chagrin. The other fire crews were working on the second house. The first house was under control and in overhaul when a horrifyingly familiar sound rent through the air. Two police officers went down, knocked flat by a terrific explosion. Protected by the bulk of the engine, Kenzie peered around the rear end. The spectators down the block were screaming in horror. A third house was blazing. Flames shot from the windows.

"Dispatch, Engine one requesting fourth alarm. Engine one requesting fourth alarm. Dispatch, roll the ladder from station two. And roll all engines from station five" The chief snatched up his radio.

"Dispatch, engine one, copy. Dispatch, station two, toning out ladder truck to 1200 block of east Mesa Drive, time is 0700... . Dispatch, station 5, roll engines five and six to 1200 block of Mesa Drive. Dispatch, station...." Kenzie no longer heard the dispatch relaying their instructions. Her entire being was focused on the burning house.

The house's front door blew off all but one hinge and hung crazily across the doorway for a moment before it flew up and out, thudding into the flowerbed. Fire followed it. Kenzie stared as the fire literally ran across the yard. The spectators' screams intensified, and she realized that the fire was a person, two legs still running under a sheet of flame. As if she watched herself from above, she saw herself whirl, wrench open a locker, and grab a blanket. Then she turned to run. For the rest of her life, Kenzie's nightmares would take this form.

Heavy boots slowing every stride. Running in slow motion. Boots seemingly sucked to the ground. The desire to vomit. The desire to run in the other direction. Sweat pouring down under her bunker coat. She smashed down the faceplate on her helmet since her facemask was still clipped to her harness. She did not have the time to stop and pull it on. Everything went blurry, but she did not need to see clearly to locate the blazing figure. Every step carried her closer, but it seemed that the figure was always just beyond reach. As she ran, she shook the blanket open. They collided, and she wrapped the blanket around the figure as they fell. Frantically, she beat the fire out. Her bunker gear and faceplate protected her from the flames but not from the smell.

Other firefighters joined her, one with an extinguisher. White foam covered her, the figure, and the smoking grass. Malone pulled Kenzie off and to the side as if she weighed nothing, and she had to scrabble in the foam-wet grass to stand up.

Malone lifted the blanket away. The figure was nothing but black char. The face had bubbled away. Eyes gone. Ears gone. Every firefighter's nightmare lay in front of them. Kenzie fought off a wave of nausea. The smell was indescribable. It would be a very long time before anyone could bear the smell of roasting meat and burning meat would trigger flashbacks. Someone vomited on the edge of Kenzie's hearing, and her stomach flipped in agreement.

"Who is it?"

"I don't know." Almost reluctantly, Malone tried to find an unburned surface to check for a pulse, pulling back the blanket to search for a surface he could touch. Fingers gone. Arms starting to pull into grotesque shapes. "Get me an ambu-bag and the first aid kit."

Glad to have something to do, but sure it was unneeded, Kenzie ran over to the rescue truck and secured the requested equipment. She brought the equipment back, and just for a moment, Malone tried to use it, but there was little point.

"He's toast." Malone flipped the blanket over the corpse's face. The awful pun in his words caught up with him, and he staggered off to be violently ill. Charred stocking cap and something else clung to the blanket. Kenzie leaned closer and touched the strands of what looked like brown hair. She staggered back with a muffled whimper.

"Get a grip. Kenzie." The Lieutenant grabbed her arm and shook it, his own face white with strain. "The media's here."

Kenzie looked at him wildly, and he shook her arm again. She nodded at his warning and walked over to the cameras and reporters. Her job was waiting. She tried speaking a few times on the way over, and by the time she was peppered with questions, her voice was under control.

"That's Tina Sarkasian's house." The reporter gestured toward the third house. "She's gonna have kittens over this."

"Good thing she's on vacation. I think the producer should have to tell her." The cameraman replied. The two snickered as they imagined the unpleasant scene awaiting someone. "So, who's the stiff?"

"What?" Kenzie started; her attention focused on the revelation. "Oh. We have to wait for positive identification and notification of next of kin. We'll have a press conference as soon as we know anything." The practiced lines rolled off her tongue. "Have you seen Gordo?" The thought occurred to her suddenly. This was the only fire she had not seen him lurking in the background, camera burning up bytes.

"Naw. Gordo's on vacation, too." The reporter replied. "Mr. Pulitzer Prize is going to be pissed about missing this one."

"Serves him right. He still seeing Tina? I'd sooner sleep with a snake, myself." The cameraman shuddered.

"Excuse me, gentlemen. I need to go get briefed myself. See you at the press conference." Kenzie nodded and walked back to the fire engine. They could find her if they needed to. Right now, there were plenty of eyewitnesses to interview.

She could never remember much of the rest of the fire. With

five engines responding and eight crews, composed of every firefighter the city and county could contact, they put all three fires out and searched every house for timing devices just waiting to incinerate another home. Two houses were a total loss, the pool was empty, and they finally had all the water they needed. The water crew finished a heroic job of reconnecting the lines just as the last house fell in smoking ruin. The coroner collected the body, so badly burned that it would require dental identification. The police found a bicycle in the alley. Kenzie could not force herself to go look at it.

They were finally finished. Every hose rolled. The fence was put back. There was no need to lock the empty swimming pool back up. It was time to go home. B and C shifts would do the overhaul. It was early evening on what had to be the longest day of her life. The reaction set in, and she was suddenly so drained she could hardly climb into the van. The step seemed too far to lift her leg. Kurt finally gave her a discreet shove in, frowning at her in worry. He pulled a granola bar from the pocket of his bunker coat.

"Blood sugar's low. Eat up." He muttered. Kenzie took the bar in both hands because they trembled. She managed to unwrap the bar and reluctantly chewed it up. She hated granola. And she was petrified she would lose it in a very undignified manner. However, Kurt had a point, and right now, he looked as if he would force-feed her if she refused.

At the firehouse, everyone showered off the stink of fire and of death. There was not the usual rehashing of the fire. Everyone seemed subdued with the horror of the day and the still fresh horror of the last death. Kenzie collected Flower and made her way home.

As Kenzie pulled into her driveway, she saw someone knocking on Lee's door. A truck with two dirt bikes loaded in the back end was idling in front of his townhouse; Lee's truck was in the driveway. Kenzie walked towards the man, pulled by an invisible thread. It was Steve, the highway patrolman, Lee's dirt biking friend.

"Hey, Kenzie." The man glanced at her and then jogged the few steps over.

"Hey, Steve."

"You know where Lee is? We were supposed to go dirt biking this morning, but he hasn't been here all day, and he's not answering his cell phone." He looked at the screen of his cell in frustration. He glanced back at her. "You alright? You look kind of sick."

"I haven't seen him... lately. I hope. Sorry." She managed to make it back to her SUV and fumbled the door open, letting Flower out. The walk to her front door seemed endless. Somewhere in the distance, she could hear Steve peppering her with questions. For a long moment, she stood at her door, trying to remember which key opened her front door. Steve finally took the keyring from her, fumbled through the different keys, and unlocked the door.

"You don't look so good. Is there someone I can call?"

Kenzie shook her head wordlessly and all but slammed the door in Steve's face. She raced up the stairs to the bathroom and threw up until there was nothing left to lose. Granola was much worse the second time around. The floor seemed a comfortable place, and she leaned her head against the cool plastic of the tub for a very long time. She showered up for the third time in an endless day, dry heaves racking her body. She managed to pull on sweats and stagger back downstairs to sit on the couch. The sun had set, and full darkness filled the house. She got up once to let Flower out, but the rest of the time, she waited. At some point, she may have slept, but she was not sure.

Dawn light lifted the shadows a little at a time, and then obscenely cheerful sunlight flooded the house—another beautiful day. Kenzie choked on a sob. Flower had kept her vigil all night, lying quietly at her feet, giving her time to see how he was aging. It would not be long until he was retired.

The sun had traced a path across the carpet from east to the zenith, and Kenzie felt as if she knew every imperfection and dog hair in the carpet's pile. She considered cleaning the carpet in a very distant fashion. It was too much effort to get up.

Flower shoved himself into a sitting position and woofed gently at the door. Kenzie shot off the couch and was at the door before the bell had even rung. For better or worse, the waiting was over. She jerked the door open. The sudden activity on top of sitting very still for a very long time made the blood rush from her head. She clung to the door handle, waiting for the darkness to clear.

"Kenzie? What's the matter? You don't look so good." She heard the voice from a long way away and reached out, grabbing the speaker by the collar and pulling him in the house. She held very tightly to Lee, crying and laughing. After a surprised moment, he gently but firmly took her by the arms and moved her away from him. Kenzie stumbled back, grasping his hand, and Lee, perforce, followed her, just enough inside the house to close the door. Kenzie reached out to touch his face. Lee stood very still for a moment. The warmth of his skin reassured her. No burns. No nightmare of charred meat. He was genuine and very safe. It was over.

"What the hell is going on?"

"It's over. Oh, thank god. It's over."

"What?" Lee sounded baffled. Kenzie wiped a few tears away and dropped her hand from his face.

"Come sit down. I'm about to collapse. I haven't eaten in about twenty-four hours. " Kenzie led him to the couch and sat down, still claiming his hand. "Where have you been? It's been all over the news. We had a hell of a day. Two days. I don't know. The arsonist struck again. This time, he torched three houses right in a row, and we're pretty sure he set himself on fire on the third one. Oh, god, it was awful, Lee. The fire he was setting flashed, and he came out of the building like a torch. I got the fire out, wrapped him in a blanket. But we were too late. He was dead."

"Did you recognize him?"

"No. He... had no face." Kenzie shuddered, her stomach heaving in memory.

"And you've been sitting here thinking it was me?" Lee drew back, pulling his hand free, but Kenzie grabbed onto his hand with both of hers.

"No." The negative blurted out before she could think. "No, no." She looked down at their hands. He had such strong, capable hands. Working hands. She had to get something to eat soon. Kenzie shook her head to clear the random thoughts that skittered, though. "I've been thinking about John. What he must have looked like. That there must be some cosmic justice, after all. You know what was really weird? The third house was.... Tina Sarkisian's."

"That's really bizarre. Tina's probably involved with this up to her scrawny neck. I wouldn't put it past her. Her and the weird photographer friend of yours. See him today?"

"The other reporters said he's on vacation."

"Really..." Lee's voice held a wealth of meaning.

"Where were you this morning, I mean yesterday morning? Steve was looking for you. Last night, I think." Kenzie asked as casually as she could.

"Oh, damn. I forgot about him." Lee frowned. "It's been two hellish days, right up there with yours. I was with my parents at the hospital all day yesterday and most of today. Dad had a heart attack."

"Oh, god, no." Kenzie stood up. Lee reached up and dragged her back to the couch.

"Sit down, Kenzie. You're not exactly someone they want to see right now. Mom recognized the symptoms and gave him some aspirin and called the hospital. I guess most of the ambulances in town were tied up with your fires. I was out biking, and she called me next. I ended up taking him to the ER."

"Is he...?"

"He's too tough to die. He got a by-pass and a whole new diet and exercise program. He's still grumbling about the diet part." Lee smiled. Kenzie's breath huffed out on a tiny laugh.

"Oh, geez. I am so glad." Kenzie bowed her head. She was very tired of crying, especially in front of Lee. He pulled out his cell phone.

"Helps if you turn the stupid thing on. Course, I couldn't get any calls in the ER or the ICU. No cells allowed... twelve messages, all from Steve. Hang on a second." He dialed the phone.

Kenzie thought for a minute about the lie she had told. Even with the evidence mounted against him, she had not really thought Lee was the arsonist. However, they could have been wrong, all of them, Bob Chu, the ATF, the police chief, her. She had had to present the evidence. It could have prevented one death... Even if it had not, and it had cost her, her best friend and her lover. At least this time, she had kept her mouth shut. And she would go to the grave with her lips sealed. Kenzie sent up a little prayer to protect her from the ravages of Alzheimer's and spilled secrets.

Lee hung up his cell phone and sat back.

"You haven't eaten?"

"Not since yesterday at the fire. I couldn't keep anything down."

"Want a pizza?" Lee asked. Kenzie laughed.

"What, your dad's heart attack didn't teach you anything? I don't think I can bear to eat meat, probably not for a very long time."

"Salad? From Renata's? Cheese bread?"

"I have some wine. It'd be a feast."

Lee searched through his phone for a moment and then ordered. Kenzie watched him in the waning light. She could see where he would have wrinkles when he was older. There was even a hint of grey above one temple. She closed her eyes for a moment or two, feeling exhaustion wash over her. With an effort, she dragged her eyes open again. Lee was watching her.

"Thank you," Kenzie whispered.

"For what?"

"For being here. For helping when... John died." Kenzie said softly. Lee shrugged.

"Just did what I'd do for anyone."

"To repeat what I said a while back, what are you doing here?"

"I thought you might want to know about Dad. It's maybe not the sort of news you pass on over the phone."

"Eh, no. Thanks for that." She closed her eyes again and felt herself slump against him. He wrapped one arm around her, snuggling her in. For the first time in a very long time, she felt herself relax and hugged him back. She pulled back and looked at him.

"Where do we go from here?" Kenzie asked quietly.

"I don't know. I'm not really sure I like you very well." Lee said, honestly. Kenzie closed her eyes against the pain. "But I have missed you. I guess we go one day at a time. One crisis at a time." Lee's voice held a hint of a laugh.

"No more crises. My nerves are shot." Kenzie mumbled.

"Yeah, well..." He reached out, pulling Kenzie back to him. She held him, head on his chest, listening to the steady thumping of his heart under her ear. He played with her hair, gently pulling out the tangles. "Let's see what happens tomorrow. This is enough for tonight."

Epilogue

Kenzie sat in her office in her favorite thinking position, feet on the desk, bouncing the ball from the wall to herself. They'd gotten the autopsy report back the week before, and Bob had leaked it to her that day, long before the media got it. It was, Kenzie thought, much to Lee's credit, that he did not gloat over the identity of the arsonist. Gordon "Gordo" Ellis, award-winning photographer, college friend, arsonist, and murderer, died in the fire. Kenzie had no tears left to shed for someone who had plotted to kill firefighters. In doing so, Gordo had wrung all her sorrow from her. Most days, she was too heart weary to even feel anger towards him.

They- the feds, the ATF, and the state fire marshal- had searched Gordo's house and had found numerous references to "the snake" but no names. It had almost been as though he were afraid of the person. Lee firmly believed that the snake was Tina, and it had all been her grand plan for revenge. Kenzie was willing to admit to the woman's need for vengeance was pathological, but to use a firebug to set up her old boyfriend whose current squeeze was a firefighter seemed overly Machiavellian and just a little too coincidental. Tina was playing the heartbroken girlfriend with great glee. Rumor had it that a bigger station was courting her with the weekend anchor spot. Kenzie truly hoped John had not died because of a jealous ex, and not even one of his own at that. It would be too ironic.

Kenzie looked up at the framed photo on the wall, Gordo's famous print of John's death. She gently reached out to touch Lee's face as the image looked forever at the frozen flames. She'd had the picture framed and hung to remind her of the price John had paid for her inability to solve the arson string. Lee had argued with her when she had first hung it up. There had been an entire team looking, and none of them had solved the arsons. Kenzie left it up, a penance for putting the wrong clues together and her silent shame over accusing Lee.

She stood up and very carefully began removing pins and markers from her city map, stowing them away in a tin. This arson was over, but there would be others.

About the Author

Marjorie Daley lives in Wyoming with her husband Bob, horse Penny, and naughty dog Diesel.

You can connect with me on:

https://fb.me/MarjorieDaleyauthor
http://marjorie-reflections.blogspot.com

Also by Marjorie Daley

The Ultimate Guide to Wild Canines, Primitive Dogs, and Pariah Dogs: An Owner's Guide Book for Wolfdogs, Coydogs, and Other Hereditarily Wild Dog Breeds

Naughty Dogs: Identifying, Diagnosing, Understanding, and Correcting Your Dog's Unwanted Behaviors